Joyeux
Noël!

De la part de :

....

Pour James Gilbert,
qui a perdu une dent le jour de Noël. – P.B.

Pour Codie et Kyle. – G.P.

Catalogage avant publication de Bibliothèque et Archives Canada

Bently, Peter, 1960-
[Tooth Fairy's Christmas. Français]
Le Noël de la fée des dents / Peter Bently ; illustrations de Garry
Parsons ; texte français d'Hélène Pilotto.

Traduction de : The Tooth Fairy's Christmas.
ISBN 978-1-4431-4033-1 (couverture souple)

I. Parsons, Garry, illustrateur II. Pilotto, Hélène, traducteur
III. Titre. IV. Titre : Tooth Fairy's Christmas. Français.

PZ23.B4574No 2015   j823'.92   C2015-900851-4

Édition publiée par les Éditions Scholastic,
604, rue King Ouest, Toronto (Ontario) M5V 1E1.

5 4 3 2 1   Imprimé à Hong Kong CP159   15 16 17 18 19

Le Noël de la fée des dents

Texte français de
HÉLÈNE PILOTTO

Illustrations de
GARRY PARSONS

PETER BENTLY

Éditions
SCHOLASTIC

C'est la veille de Noël. La neige tombe à n'en plus finir.
La fée des dents reçoit une lettre et pousse un long soupir.

— Moi qui pensais passer la soirée au chaud,
je dois récupérer la dent de Timothé Michot.

Sitôt dehors, le vent la pousse

de tous bords tous côtés.

Il emporte son bonnet et gonfle sa jupe colorée.

Transie de froid, la fée est secouée de frissons.   Au bout de son nez

se forme un glaçon.

— Flûte de flûte! Je suis complètement perdue à présent!
soupire la fée en secouant la neige de ses vêtements.

Oh! Mais... qu'est-ce que j'aperçois là-haut?
Cet objet volant... ce bruit de grelots...
Cela ressemble...

— **Bonsoir!** clame le père Noël. Tu en fais une tête!
Pourquoi es-tu dehors un soir de grande tempête?
— J'apporte un cadeau à Timothé Michot, mais j'ai perdu mon chemin!
— Monte! répond le vieil homme. Nous y serons en un tournemain!

Arrivés chez Timothé, ils constatent que la cheminée est bloquée.

— Bon sang! s'écrie le père Noël. Et toutes les portes sont verrouillées!

— Laissez-moi faire, dit la fée des dents avec un sourire radieux. Il y a une fente dans cette fenêtre. Nous allons entrer en moins de deux!

Elle agite sa baguette et dit : « MAGIE-FLEXI-BULLE! »

Et les voilà tous deux à l'intérieur d'une bulle,

qui rapetisse et prend la taille d'un petit pois, puis disparaît dans la fente en un claquement de doigts.

La bulle éclate devant la chambre de l'enfant…

POP!

Les deux passagers retrouvent leur taille immédiatement.

Il fait si noir dans la chambre de Timothé
que la fée doit aider le père Noël à s'orienter.
— Attention, lui chuchote-t-elle, il y a un
train tout près du lit!

En voulant l'éviter, le vieux bonhomme écrase
un jouet et fait du bruit.

La fée des dents songe :
« Dors, petit garçon. »
Puis elle volette jusqu'à l'oreiller
de Tim avec précaution.

Elle dépose une pièce en échange de la dent,

puis murmure au père Noël : « Rentrons à présent. »

Contents

1
The Basic Idea

Whether a veteran cook or a beginner, your responsibility is to prepare food for the best possible nutrition and palatability. After all, most people eat what they *like*, good for them or not. Contrary to the Puritan legend that what is good for you must be endured, good nutrition and palatability are not mutually exclusive. Properly cooked meat is more tender and succulent; it is also more digestible, and its amino acids become more available to the body. A white bread with higher protein, vitamin, and mineral values tastes better than the "bubblegum" commercial variety. Homemade cake with elevated nutritional value can make the product of a cake mix taste like what it is: a triumph of the chemist over common sense, of the processor over the laws of nature. Properly cooked vegetables are more nutritious, and taste better for it.

The "best possible nutrition" is a phrase with built-in, hidden traps. Best possible for whom? Man's heredity varies, and his nutritional needs with it. On a uniform diet, chickens of the same heredity don't turn out the same. Some grow slowly, some faster; some are sickly, others function; some are superbly healthy; most live, some die. The chicken eats what is available; man, what pleases him. Unfortunately, man seems no better able to detect the relationship between his diet and his health than does the chicken (it has been said that the last discovery made by a deep-sea fish would be salt water).

The broiler of today reaches marketing weight in a fraction of the time it took thirty years ago. Yet the poultry scientists of that day were sure they knew practically everything about feeding fowl, exactly as our nutritionists today write about human nutrition, with the assurance that all knowledge is at hand, and all members of a species have the same nutritional requirements.

Before World War II, the Japanese accepted their shortness as an hereditary trait. Now with their children growing taller than their parents, the Japanese realize that their prewar short stature was an adaptation of their bodies to limitations in the national diet. Yet Japanese nutritionists of the 1930s were quite sure they knew all the major answers to questions about human dietary needs. Which brings into sharp focus the attempt of our Food and Drug Administration to *legislate* a uniform requirement for vitamins and all other nutrients needed by two hundred million Americans.

A half-ounce cake of compressed yeast, given good nutrition continuously, would grow to a billion tons in *one* week. Do our yeast growers provide such a balanced diet for these cells (assuming that all varieties have the same requirements, which they don't)? Don't be silly: we'd be up to our ears in yeast, instead of having intermittent shortages. Yet our knowledge of the nutritional needs of yeast is more detailed and complete than our understanding of the much more complicated requirements of man. Moreover, yeast doesn't scramble its genes as does man with haphazard mating; nor complicate matters by requiring a restricted diet for allergies; nor insist, as we do, on consuming foods with additives known to interfere with efficient reproduction. (Your very vitamin pills are probably colored with some kind of additive. It is also found in most lipsticks.)

Question: how do you know your nutrition is not—in some subtle or even in some explicit ways—forcing your body, your nervous system, or your brain into a compromise, an adaptation to an unfavorable internal environment such as the Japanese unknowingly made? How do you know what kind of chicken you are? What makes you sure, if you *are* sure, that your sicknesses are not related to your choices and methods of preparation of foods? The U.S. Department of Agriculture has made up its mind: "Up to 90 percent of our common diseases," their literature flatly states, "could be mitigated or wiped out, if we ate properly."

How do you know that your child's hyperactivity is not a direct price for the artificial colors and flavors in the convenience foods you have innocently served? A recent report blamed a drug action of these chemicals for the hyperactivity which in some states impairs the functioning and the educability of up to 40 percent of our school children. It disappeared, the American Medical Association was informed, when the chemicals were eliminated from their diets, and reappeared when they were reintroduced. Questions: do you read the fine print on the labels of your favorite brands of foods? With understanding?

Finally, how do you *know* that you don't fall short of meeting your nutritional requirements and those of your family, exactly as the yeast growers and the chicken breeders fall short of providing the ideal nutritional environment for the living cells they feed? Before you answer: one of my professional friends, a fine medical nutritionist, made a small improvement in the diets of eight hundred professional men and their families. It resulted in a measurable improvement in their mental and emotional functioning—yet they all considered themselves to be at least reasonably well fed before the research began—and theirs were typical American diets of affluent families. The removal of one single food from the diet of a "neurotic hypochondriac" woman restored her normal cheerful personality, her psychiatrist—an orthomolecular practitioner, using nutrition instead of the couch—reported. Removal of much of the sugar from the diets of school children not only dramatically lowered tooth decay but their rate of illness also declined, and their school grades rose; yet their parents had thought them "well fed." So the question: are your food choices intelligent? is not an idle one. And in your preparation of your meals, which can make a tremendous difference in their nutritional values, are you retaining vital nutrients, or throwing the baby out with the bath water?

All this distinctly doesn't mean munching on raw foods, though there is a place in your menus for some which are delightful and healthful. It doesn't commit you to drinking alfalfa juice laced with blackstrap molasses. There's nothing wrong with health foods, but something very wrong with the concept that foods good for you must be exotic, unpalatable, and the choice only of little old ladies in tennis shoes. All foods are supposed to be healthful to the degree that they supply the body's requirements. All additives should be harmless, and all processing innocent of negative effects on food values, and both should fulfill a function benefiting the consumer. Unhealthful additives and harmful processing should be stopped, and will be, if you exercise your ballot in the market place.

It is obvious that I am a nutritionist with very definite ideas about what you should eat to improve your diet. It is equally true that you are a peace-loving homemaker with a family with very definite ideas about what it *will* eat. Put your mind at rest: I am a nutritionist who will settle for less than the millennium—for the good reason that experience has taught me its unattainability. I have learned that it is wiser (and more effective) to outflank the family's resistance, rather than attack it head-on. That leads to Rule #1 (and 2 and 3): never place a dish or a meal before your husband and the children, and announce that it's (a) a new one, and (b) good for them. Eating things that are good for one is taking care of one's self. That is essentially a feminine philosophy, which is why this book is addressed to you. American men, doubtful about their masculinity, suffer great anxiety when asked to participate in something they consider feminine. They therefore are charter-bound to reject anything that is good for them. So you are, from this point on, a happy participant in a conspiracy between good nutrition and you.

If you are a modern homemaker with a sincere desire to provide your family with good nutrition, you should read carefully the following discussions about vegetable and meat cookery before proceeding to the recipe sections. This is especially recommended if you are a beginner, or if you learned to cook peering from behind your mother's apron or into cookbooks made obsolete by contemporary needs, the quality of contemporary foods, and revised or new concepts about preserving food nutrients.

Mother may have been the best cook in the world, but her cooking methods and her ideas about food were not geared to modern nutritional knowledge or requirements. Think back to the dinners of your childhood, or reread some of her cherished recipes (inherited, probably, from the best cook in the world of her generation—your grandmother). Do you find instructions to sear the meat invariably—to roast it in a very hot oven—to drown it in flour gravy—to boil vegetables for a long time, adding baking soda to "retain color"?

Among the facts to emerge from modern scientific nutrition test kitchens is one which reveals that ordinary, old-fashioned cooking methods may mean the loss of up to 95 percent of the vitamins and minerals in certain foods. Even under ideal conditions, cooking often subtracts sizable percentages of nutrients from foods' assayed raw values—one reason why you will find, in this cookbook, the use of special-purpose foods as recipe ingredients. They are introduced to help offset losses which may have occurred in the raising or processing of food, or in cooking.

For many women, the following instructions may mean discarding long-held habits and acquiring new ones. If you have been accustomed to cooking methods which contradict mine, there is a very good chance that you have been innocently depriving your family of vitamins, minerals, and proteins—as well as flavor—in the meals you serve.

Vegetable Cookery

On the subject of vegetable cookery I am stubborn. There is no separate chapter in this book with lots of lovely recipes reading from *artichokes* to *zucchini*, although there are plenty of recipes using vegetables as ingredients. Vegetables taste fine just the way they are—some of them raw, others briefly cooked to permit the retention of their color and flavor and a decent amount of whatever vitamins and minerals they were born with. Anything elaborate you do to them is likely to demand more exposure to light, air, and heat (all nutrient robbers) than I care to think about.

Cook the freshest vegetables you can find in the following ways: Steaming, pressure-cooking, sautéing, broiling, or baking; creaming them when half-cooked in a sauce to which you add extra nutrients (milk, milk solids, cheese, wheat germ, yeast flakes); simmering them in milk and using the milk; or cooking them very quickly in an absolute minimum of water and using the water. They should be cooked only until they are tender, not soft, and not a second longer.

Frozen vegetables are preferred to "fresh" varieties which may have suffered nutrient losses owing to premature harvesting, transportation, and storage or display without refrigeration. Because frozen vegetables are partially precooked at the source to arrest enzymic action and "lock in" nutritive value, flavor, and texture, follow carefully the producers' instructions, printed on the packages, to cook them briefly.

If family palates or prejudices insist that vegetables be embellished as an alternative to being uneaten, then for goodness' sake do it in such a way as to add nutrition, not subtract it.

A fine embellishment is lemon juice, for it replaces some of the easily destroyed vitamin C which starts vanishing as soon as a vegetable is wrenched from earth, stalk, or vine.

Excellent would be a judicious addition of wheat germ or yeast flakes for the sake of B vitamins and vitamin E, lacking in many of the foods you eat.

Simmering in milk is good, because milk adds its protein and calcium and is in less danger of being thrown away than water.

Creamy sauces made with unbleached or whole-wheat flour, with or without cheese, have nutritional value—but perhaps they are best avoided unless someone at your house is on a weight-gaining diet or won't drink milk straight in the recommended quantity. Aside from adding more calories than you probably need, heavy sauces take up too much appetite room to be considered wholly desirable.

Whenever possible, dice, slice, or shred vegetables. They'll cook faster, keeping nutrient losses to a minimum. Also, whenever possible, prepare and cook vegetables just before serving and try to cook only as much as will be eaten during the meal for which they are intended. If any are left over, refrigerate or freeze them without delay.

Meat Cookery

If you still cook meat without using a meat thermometer, I shall pause long enough for you to run out and buy one. From now on, any meat you cook "plain" by braising, broiling, pan-broiling, roasting, or sautéing (the preferred methods) will be certain of success, both gastronomic and nutritional, if you serve it when the proper thermometer reading is reached and provided you *take the time to cook meat slowly, at low temperatures.*

Braise meat over low range heat or in a low oven.

Broil meat at a low temperature if your broiler has a heat control; if not, place meat to be broiled from 4 to 6 inches from the source of heat.

Pan-broil meat over low range heat.

Roast at low (300°) temperature, unless the recipe specifies otherwise. If your oven is not equipped with an accurate oven thermometer, buy one and use it as directed by the manufacturer, using also your meat thermometer.

Sauté over low range heat.

An Explanation of Recommended Meat Cookery Terms

Braise: To Cook by Steam

Less tender cuts of meat retain flavor and nutrients if carefully braised. Brown the meat on all sides in a heavy utensil—slowly, over low heat, without adding fat. To intensify browning and add flavor in some recipes, the meat may first be dredged with whole-wheat flour; in this case, it is necessary to add a small amount of oil or fat to the pan. When the meat is browned, place it on a rack in a heavy utensil which can be covered tightly. Add a small amount of liquid (stock or vegetable water), cover closely, and cook over low heat until tender or for time specified in recipe. A little lemon juice or vinegar added to the liquid shortens cooking time and acts as a tenderizer. Braising may also be done in a very low (200°) oven. Brown as directed, place on rack, add liquid and lemon juice or vinegar, cover closely, and set in a slow oven until meat is tender and proper thermometer reading is reached.

Broil: To Cook by Exposing Meat Directly to Heat

To broil successfully, do not preheat broiling compartment. Keep heat low, if your broiler has a temperature control, and place meat on the top rack. If your broiler has no temperature control, place meat from 4 to 6 inches from the source of heat. Leave broiler door open. Broil one side for half the total cooking time; turn meat, insert meat thermometer, and finish cooking to state of desired doneness (rare, medium, or well done) according to proper thermometer reading.

Pan-broil: To Cook in a Pan over Direct Heat

Place meat in a heavy skillet without adding fat or water. Do not cover. Turn occasionally, and pour off or remove fat as it accumulates. Cook over low heat for amount of time specified in recipe.

Roast: To Cook by Surrounding Meat with Dry Heat

Place meat, fat side up, on a rack in an open shallow roasting pan. Insert a meat thermometer so that its bulb is in the center of the largest muscle. The bulb should not touch bone or rest in fat. Add no water, and do not cover. Roast at oven temperature specified for the amount of time given in the recipe, or until thermometer reading indicates the state of doneness at which you wish to serve the meat (rare, medium, well done).

Sauté: To Cook in a Minimum of Fat

Add to pan only enough oil or fat to prevent food from sticking. Meat may be dredged with whole-wheat flour or whole-wheat bread crumbs, or it may be sautéed without dredging. Start cooking meat over moderate heat, sear for only 1 or 2 minutes on each side, reduce heat to low (or remove pan to a low unit, if you use an electric range), and continue cooking over low heat for amount of time specified in recipe.

Recommended Cooking Methods, Times, and Temperatures for Meat and Poultry*

Note: The cooking times given in the following table apply only to meat and poultry at room temperature. Allow more time if chilled. Frozen meats or poultry should be defrosted before cooking.

Cut	Cooking Method	Time to Allow	Oven Temperature or Surface Heat
		MEAT	
Beef:			
Standing or rolled rib roast	Roast	Rare: 18–20 min. per lb. Medium: 22–25 min. per lb. Well done: 27–32 min. per lb.	300°
Round, rump, or chuck roast	Roast	Rare: 45–50 min. per lb. Medium: 55–60 min. per lb. Well done: 60–70 min. per lb.	250°
	Braise	60 min. per lb.	Very low (simmer)
Steaks, tender cuts (sirloin, porterhouse, T-bone, club)	Broil	*2-in. steaks* Rare: 30–40 min. Medium: 45–50 min. *1-in. steaks* Rare: 25–30 min. Medium: 35–40 min. *½-in. steaks* Rare: 12–15 min. Medium: 17–20 min.	Low, 4 in. from source of heat
Steaks, less tender cuts (chuck, round)	Broil	*1-in. steaks* Rare: 35–45 min. Medium: 45–50 min. *½-in. steaks* Rare: 18–20 min. Medium: 22–25 min.	Very low, 5–6 in. from source of heat
Ham:			
Whole or half	Roast	25–30 min. per lb.	300°
Tenderized	Roast	20–25 min. per lb.	300°

Unless otherwise specified in individual recipes.

Cut	Cooking Method	Time to Allow	Oven Temperature or Surface Heat
Ham: continued			
Steaks:			
Not tenderized	Broil or pan-broil	*1-in. steaks* 40–45 min. *½-in. steaks* 20–25 min.	Low, 4 in. from source of broiler heat, or over low heat on range
Tenderized	Broil or pan-broil	*1-in. steaks* 20–30 min. *½-in. steaks* 15–20 min.	
Lamb:			
Leg	Roast	25–30 min. per lb.	300°
Shoulder	Roast	40–45 min. per lb.	275°
Breast	Roast	30–35 min. per lb.	300°
Chops or steaks	Broil	*2-in. chops* 40–45 min. *1-in. chops or steaks* 20–30 min.	Low, 4 in. from source of broiler heat
Pork:			
Loin cuts	Roast	35–40 min. per lb.	300°
Shoulder	Roast	40–45 min. per lb.	300°
Fresh ham	Roast	35–40 min. per lb.	300°
Chops	Broil (be sure to use meat thermometer)	*1½-in. chops* 40–45 min.	Low, 4 in. from source of broiler heat
	Pan-broil	*1-in. chops* 30–35 min.	Low heat on range
Veal:			
Leg	Roast	25–30 min. per lb.	300°
Loin	Roast	30–35 min. per lb.	300°
Shoulder	Roast	40–45 min. per lb.	300°
Chops (¾-1 in.)	Braise	45–50 min.	Low heat on range
Cutlets (½-in.)	Braise	30–35 min.	Low heat on range

POULTRY

Cut	Cooking Method	Time to Allow	Oven Temperature or Surface Heat
Chicken:			
Parts	Broil, pan-broil, sauté	45–50 min.	Low, 4 in. from source of broiler heat, or over low heat on range
Whole	Roast	35–40 min. per lb.	300°

Cut	Cooking Method	Time to Allow	Oven Temperature or Surface Heat
Turkey:			
Small (8–13 lb.)	Roast	20–25 min. per lb.	300°
Large (14 lb. or over)	Roast	15–18 min. per lb.	300°
Duck	Roast	25–30 min. per lb.	300°
Goose	Roast	25–30 min. per lb.	300°

Throughout this cookbook, whenever other cooking methods are used—as for stews, meat loaves and patties, casseroles, etc.—specific cooking times and temperatures are given. All organ meat recipes also include specific instructions.

Why Special-Purpose Foods?

In many recipes in this cookbook, you will note several special ingredients with which you may or may not be familiar, for example: wheat germ, wheat-germ oil, brewers' yeast, yeast flakes, skim-milk solids, monosodium glutamate, sugarless sweeteners, soybeans or soybean flour, whole-wheat pastry flour, etc. My students and listeners to the "Living Should Be Fun" broadcasts are aware of the nutritional values of these special-purpose foods. For those to whom emphasis on good nutrition is a new idea in home cookery, let me say briefly here that these are foods whose contributions to diet cannot be overstated. They provide protective amounts of proteins, vitamins, and minerals much needed in modern diets.

Where To Find Special-Purpose Foods

Happily, as emphasis on good nutrition for good health continues to grow in schools, medical research laboratories, government agencies, and the public awareness, the special-purpose foods mentioned throughout this book are becoming more and more available from more and more sources. There was a time, not too many years ago, when you would have had to go to a farmers' feed and grain store to find blackstrap molasses, to a brewery for brewers' yeast, to flour mills for wheat-germ and whole-grain flours and cereals, to the military quartermaster or a dairy farm for skim-milk solids.

While some of the special flours and other items must still be sought out, most of the special-purpose foods can be found on the shelves of your favorite supermarket. If your store does not have them, ask the manager to stock them and persuade your friends and neighbors to request them also. These foods are—or soon will be—commercially available and nationally distributed. The housewives of America may not realize it fully, but they are the ones who determine to a large extent what foods, of what quality, are offered by the retailers. If there is sufficient demand for special-purpose foods, your local merchants will be happy to stock them.

For your general guidance, suggested sources for special-purpose foods are given below. When more than one source is given, the listing (reading from left to right) is in an order indicating the most reliable and usually the most realistically priced sources.

Banana flakes: Food chain and independent grocery stores; drugstores.

Brewers' yeast: Leading mail-order vitamin firms; drug stores; breweries;* health food stores.

Special note about brewers' yeast: Yeasts vary tremendously in nutritional values—particularly protein and the B Complex vitamins. They also vary in taste, from awful to quite palatable. As a starter, try Delecta yeast for incorporation in most recipes. Where a bacon flavor is acceptable, try Bakon Yeast. Both are available in health food stores.

Cereals, whole grain, no sugar added: Many varieties to be found in food chain and independent grocery stores. Otherwise—at independent local mills;* local and state farmers' exchanges;* organic gardening clubs;* health food stores.

Flour, unbleached: Food chain and independent grocery stores.

Flour, 100 percent whole wheat: Occasionally to be found at food chain and independent grocery stores. Otherwise—see next listing.

Flour, whole rye, buckwheat, soybean, potato, whole-wheat pastry: Independent local mills;* large milling companies;* local or state farmers' exchanges;* organic gardening clubs;* health food stores.

Gelatin, whole or natural, unsweetened: Food chain and independent grocery stores, health food stores.

Macaroni products, made with wheat germ and containing 20 percent protein: Food chain and independent grocery stores, health food stores.

Monosodium glutamate: Under various brand names, in food chain and independent grocery stores. Otherwise—leading mail-order vitamin firms; drugstores; health food stores.

Rice, brown or converted: Food chain and independent grocery stores; independent local mills;* health food stores.

Skim-milk solids (nonfat dry milk, nonfat milk powder): Food chain and independent grocery stores.

Sugarless sweeteners: Under various brand names, at food chain or independent grocery stores, usually on shelves where dietetic foods are displayed; drugstores; health food stores.

Undegerminated corn meal: See "Cereals, whole grain, no sugar added."

Wheat germ: Food chain and independent grocery stores; independent local mills;* milling companies;* organic gardening clubs;* health-food stores. (Defatted wheat germ has lost its saturated fat and Vitamin E. It is a good food, but inferior to natural wheat germ. Buy natural wheat germ in vacuum packing, if possible; like all good foods it is perishable.)

Wheat-germ oil: Leading mail-order vitamin firms; drugstores; health food stores.

Yeast flakes: See "Brewers' yeast."

Special note about salt: Although the recipes in this book do not specify it, the author sincerely hopes that all table and cooking salt used in your home is *iodized* unless contraindicated by a physician. Iodized salt is available in all food stores.

Special note about labels on food packages: Learn to read labels carefully. Food packagers are required to list ingredients. No product is 100 percent whole grain unless the label states that it is. No product contains wheat germ or any other special nutrient unless it is specified on the label. Salt and/or sugar additions are stated. Artificial flavorings and colorings are similarly identified, as are preservatives.

*Consult the yellow pages of your telephone book, or write to the sales department of a firm producing the end commercial product—beer, flour, macaroni, etc. Your country or state farm bureau or the agricultural department of a nearby college or university can usually supply you with a list of your area's organic farms, distributors of organically grown produce, and mills offering whole-grain cereals and flours for sale.

2
Good Nutrition
Starts the Day Right

The Importance of Breakfast

Holding this book in your hands makes you one of two kinds of people. You're either a seeker after good nutrition, or you're a cook book fan. If the former, and especially if you are familiar with my broadcasts, you won't be surprised by nonconformity. If the latter, you will find that in this cook book not only are the ideas and recipes unorthodox, but also their sequence.

By raising the curtain on breakfast, the author hopes to hold your attention long enough to convert you and your family into a group of virtuous breakfasters, eating good, nutritious, body-sustaining breakfasts instead of the little glass of fruit juice, piece of buttered toast, and cup of sweetened coffee, which masquerade as a morning meal in most households.

Good-Nutrition Cereals

If you are in the habit of feeding your family the average packaged cold breakfast cereal, you should be interested in the following account of a visit to one of this country's celebrated breakfast-food factories. Although the cereal described here is cornflakes, the procedure is essentially the same for all cold cereals not specifically labeled "whole grain."

First I saw machinery removing the outer coat, then the germ (in other words, the life) from corn. This, my guide explained, was to prevent their cornflakes from "rancidity and spoilage." He said they sent the discarded husks to "fox farms and other places where they feed animals." What was left of the corn at this point was of an unlifelike pallor as befits any corpse. Masses of this corpselike substance (I refuse to call it corn) were put in large pressure cookers, heated to a temperature of 250 degrees and held at that temperature for two and a half hours when it was ready to be mixed with artificial flavoring and coloring to make it look and taste less like the corpse it really was. The entire mass was then cooled until it reached a stage at which it was ready to be run through machines to flake it. At this point it began a journey on endless belts that passed it through heaters where it reached a temperature of 450 degrees, thus assuring loss or deterioration of nutritional elements that might have survived up to this point. The process set the flakes to prevent them from sticking together. Now it was ready for packaging in wax-paper lined cartons. This, said the guide, would keep their product "as fresh as a daisy." The factory was sending out sixty-five carloads of this foodless pap and other breakfast foods every day to be eaten by human beings. A tank car full of corn germ oil left . . . every month for the pharmaceutical houses. The little foxes got the rest of it.*

*From Open Door to Health, by Fred D. Miller, The Devin-Adair Company, New York, 1959.

With the foregoing in mind, you may want with all your heart to revise your cold-cereal purchasing but anticipate objections from your habit-inured family. Until you can persuade your housemates to accept a morning bowlful of entirely whole-grain cereal I suggest you:

1. Read labels. Avoid cereals to which sugar has been added.
2. To each serving of cereal add 1 or 2 teaspoons of wheat germ.
3. Mix customary cereal with equal portions of whole-grain types.
4. Add 2 tablespoons skim-milk solids to each cup of milk served with cereal.
5. Sweeten cereal with honey, dark molasses, or banana flakes. If you cannot turn a deaf ear to pleas for sugar, fill the sugar bowl with brown sugar.

Cooked Cereals

Granular Whole Wheat, Undegerminated Cornmeal, Quick-Cooking Oats

In water:

2 cups water	honey, molasses,
1 cup cereal	brown sugar, or
1 tsp. salt	banana flakes

In heavy saucepan with tight-fitting lid, bring water to a rolling boil over high heat. Add cereal slowly as water continues to boil, and stir briskly, adding salt. Reduce heat to gentle boil, cover tightly, and cook for 5 to 7 minutes. Add honey, dark molasses, brown sugar, or banana flakes to taste when served. *Serves 2.*

In milk:

2 cups milk	½ tsp. salt
2 Tbs. skim-milk	honey, molasses, or
solids	brown sugar
1 cup cereal	

Combine milk and milk solids and heat to simmer stage. Add cereal very slowly to prevent cooling of milk. Add salt, cover, and simmer for 5 minutes. Add honey, dark molasses, or brown sugar to taste when served. *Serves 2.*

Whole Wheat, Whole Buckwheat, Whole Grits, Rolled Oats

In water:

3 cups water	honey, molasses, or
1 cup cereal	brown sugar
1 tsp. salt	

Bring water to rolling boil, add cereal slowly as water continues to boil, and stir briskly. Add salt, reduce heat to gentle boil, cover tightly, and cook for 10 to 15 minutes. Add honey, dark molasses, or brown sugar to taste when served. *Serves 2.*

In milk:

2 cups milk	½ tsp. salt
2 Tbs. skim-milk	honey, molasses, or
solids	brown sugar
1 cup cereal	

Combine milk and milk solids and heat to simmer stage. Add cereal very slowly to prevent cooling of milk. Add salt, cover, and simmer for 10 to 15 minutes. Add honey, dark molasses, or brown sugar to taste when served. *Serves 2.*

Note: For even better nutrition and very slight variation in taste, add to each cup of dry cereal before cooking 1 teaspoon brewers' yeast or yeast flakes.

Special Cornmeal Recipes

Scrapple

If you're going to take the trouble to prepare this excellent source of protein and vitamins, you might as well make a lot. It can be stored in a refrigerator freezing compartment for three months, in a full freezer for six months. Before freezing, however, be sure to slice chilled scrapple into individual serving pieces and separate them with double thicknesses of cellophane. Wrap and seal securely.

To make 4 pounds of scrapple:

2½ lbs. ground	1 tsp. salt
pork—or 2 lbs.	½ tsp. pepper
pork and ½ pound	2 qts. water
pork liver	

Cover meat with water and add seasonings. Bring to a boil, reduce heat, and simmer for 2 hours. Remove and grind or shred meat. Strain cooking water and remove 2 cups of it, allowing it to cool. Continue to simmer remaining broth—very slowly, and well covered.

Blend together:

2 cups undeger-	1 tsp. salt
minated yellow	½ tsp. pepper
cornmeal	1 tsp. sage or savory
¾ cup wheat germ	dash cayenne

To this blend add the 2 cups of cooled broth, gradually. Keep it from lumping. When smooth, add slowly to the simmering broth, stirring constantly. Still stirring, add the ground or shredded meat. If you use an electric stove, reduce heat to lowest temperature. If you use a gas range, place pan on a low flame covered with an asbestos mat. Continue to cook slowly for 2 hours, stirring occasionally. Pour into long, narrow pans which have been rinsed in cold water. Let stand in a cool place until firm. To serve: Heat slices over moderate heat in skillet with only enough oil or shortening to prevent sticking.

Fluffy Buttermilk Spoon Bread

1 qt. buttermilk	⅓ cup wheat germ
4 Tbs. skim-milk solids	1½ tsp. salt
⅔ cup undegerminated yellow corn meal	2 Tbs. butter or margarine
	4 eggs

Combine buttermilk and skim-milk solids and heat in top of double boiler. Do not boil. Mix cornmeal, salt, and wheat germ and add to milk, stirring until thickened and smooth. Cover, reduce heat, and let cook while you pre-heat oven to 425°. Remove from heat and add butter. In large bowl beat eggs until light and frothy. Stir eggs into cornmeal mixture, blending well. Pour into well-greased baking dish and bake 50 minutes to 1 hour. Serve hot, topped with sliced fruit, honey, or maple syrup.

Banana Spoon Bread

2½ cups water	1½ cups milk
½ cup undegerminated yellow corn meal	3 Tbs. skim-milk solids
½ cup wheat germ	2 egg whites, beaten stiff
2 Tbs. butter, melted	1 cup mashed banana or ¼–½ cup banana flakes
¾ tsp. salt	
2 egg yolks, lightly beaten	

Using top of double boiler, bring water to boil over direct heat. Combine cornmeal and wheat germ and stir into boiling water. Set boiler top in its bottom part filled to proper level with boiling water. Cook 15 minutes over boiling water, remove from heat while you preheat oven to 425°. When mixture is slightly cooled, add butter, salt, egg yolks, and milk (combined with milk solids) and beat for 2 minutes with rotary or electric beater at low speed. Fold in stiffly beaten egg whites and banana pulp or flakes and pour into greased 2-quart baking dish. Bake 40 minutes.

Good-Nutrition Pancakes and Waffles

Pancakes and waffles can be as nutritious as they are seductive to early-morning appetite laggards.

It is a temptation, in this day of food processors who do everything for the busy housewife except set the table and wash the dishes, to buy a prepared pancake or waffle mix which requires only that you add liquid and introduce the stove. There are, happily, some mixes available which make an honest effort to charge their ingredients with good nutrition, and the thoughtful homemaker can serve these with a clear conscience.

For nutritional security and creative satisfaction, you should prefer to make your own batters.* Inasmuch as a genuine breakfast may almost constitute a new habit for you and your family, perhaps I can get you to put into those batters a strong dose of important B vitamins, a certain amount of vitamin E, and a nice margin of proteins. (I am assuming that fruit and fruit juices will provide a morning portion of the vitamin C you must have daily, and hoping that—in time—you will be using the bread section in this book to give meaning to carbohydrate intake.)

You will note in the recipes to follow that whenever baking powder or (rarely) baking soda is included as a concession to the morning rush, there is also mention of a generous amount of skim-milk solids, wheat germ, and brewers' yeast or yeast flakes. Let me tell you why, lest you dismiss the subject too lightly in the belief that eggs and milk are enough, or that these products are fad foods and therefore expendable.

For one thing, there are natural B vitamins in yeast you literally get from no other source in quite the same balance. Wheat germ and

---

There are a few pancake mixes available that are nutritious, and which are not seasoned with chemicals of dubious safety. Most of these are in the health food stores. Occasionally, there is a brand in the supermarkets. Read labels carefully.

wheat-germ oil supply valuable unsaturated fatty acids and vitamin E, inadequately present in most modern foods. For another thing, there is an alkali in baking soda and to a lesser degree in baking powder which destroys a high percentage of the B vitamins in the recipe ingredients milk, flour, and shortening. Extra milk solids, a yeast product, and wheat germ in your breakfast menus offset the loss—the milk solids by providing complete proteins which neutralize the alkali, and the yeast and wheat germ by providing more B vitamins than the baking powder can destroy.

Pancakes

Use a very heavy griddle or skillet and make it ready by heating it slowly. When it is properly hot, a few drops of water will sputter and bounce on the griddle surface. For the most part, a heavy enough griddle requires no greasing—or, at most, a very light coating of oil. Some cooks like to rub the griddle with a salt-filled cheesecloth bag or an oiled cloth, cleaning it also this way between uses.

To be sure of good results, batter should be medium, not thick, and not too thin. Milk can be added to batters that seem too thick, and extra wheat germ to those that are too thin.

Pour batter from a pitcher, or drop it by the spoonful onto the hot griddle, baking no more than 3 or 4 pancakes at a time. Turn pancakes only once—when bubbles break on the uncooked surface and the edges appear slightly dry, usually in 2 or 3 minutes. After you have flipped them with a wide spatula or pancake turner, the second side will brown nicely in about 1 minute.

If possible, serve pancakes at once on heated plates rather than stacking them and keeping them warm.

Apple Cinnamon Pancakes

1¼ cups unbleached or whole-wheat flour	¼ cup wheat germ
	½ tsp. cinnamon
	1 Tbs. brown sugar
1 tsp. baking powder	1½ Tbs. butter or margarine, melted
(1–2 Tbs. brewers' yeast or yeast flakes)	2 eggs, beaten
	1 cup finely chopped apples (or applesauce)
2 Tbs. skim-milk solids	1 cup milk

Combine dry ingredients, mixing well. Add melted butter, beaten eggs, and apples and blend thoroughly. Stir in milk gradually to make a smooth batter. *Makes about 16 pancakes.*

Bacon and Egg Corncakes

1 cup water	1 tsp. baking powder
1 cup undegerminated yellow cornmeal	(1–2 Tbs. brewers' yeast or yeast flakes)
2 Tbs. bacon fat	(2 Tbs. skim-milk solids)
½ cup chopped bacon	1 egg, beaten
¼ cup unbleached or whole-wheat flour	1 cup milk or buttermilk
¼ cup wheat germ	

Pour boiling water over cornmeal in a bowl and let stand while you fry chopped bacon slowly until crisp. Pour off bacon fat, reserving 2 tablespoons. Combine dry ingredients and mix with softened cornmeal. Stir in 2 tablespoons bacon fat, beaten egg, and milk. Add crisp bacon and mix thoroughly. *Makes about 16 corncakes.*

Oatmeal Pancakes

1½ cups milk	2 Tbs. wheat germ
2 cups oats	(1–2 Tbs. brewers' yeast)
⅓ cup oil	
2 eggs, beaten	(2–3 Tbs. skim-milk solids)
⅓ cup unbleached flour	

Heat but do not boil milk, and pour over oats and shortening. Cool slightly. Add and beat in eggs. Add and blend in remaining ingredients, mixing thoroughly. *Makes about 12 pancakes.*

Whole-Grain Yeast Pancakes

1 cake fresh yeast, or 1 package dry yeast	1 cup whole-wheat or whole-buckwheat flour
1½ cups warm milk	½ cup wheat germ
1 Tbs. molasses, honey, or brown sugar	(¼ cup skim-milk solids)
	1 tsp. salt
2 eggs, beaten	
2 Tbs. shortening, melted	

Stir yeast into warm milk and let stand 10 minutes. Stir in sweetener, beaten eggs, and shortening. Combine dry ingredients and stir into liquid. Mix thoroughly. Batter may be used immediately, may be allowed to rise in a warm place for 30 minutes to an hour, or may be prepared before bedtime and stored overnight in the refrigerator. *Makes 12 to 16 pancakes.*

Sour-dough Pancakes

These deserve special mention. I have taken some nutritional liberties with the traditional sour dough as it was thrown together by gold prospectors in Alaska and the old West. They, of course, knew nothing about wheat germ as a separate ingredient—their flour sometimes contained it.

To make the sour-dough starter: Peel, dice, and boil four or five potatoes until they are soft. Reserve the potatoes for some other use—it's the water you need.

2 cups warm potato water	1 tsp. salt
2 cups unbleached flour	1 yeast cake, crumbled, or 1 package dry yeast
1 Tbs. sugar	

Mix these ingredients and put them in a crock. Cover loosely and let stand in a warm place overnight or for 2 days, until the starter is "working" and giving off a yeasty, somewhat sourish smell. It is then ready for use.

Mix together in a bowl and let stand overnight in a warm place:

2 cups sour-dough starter	1 cup water
1 cup unbleached flour	

Add to bowl:

¼ cup wheat germ	1 egg, lightly beaten
¼ cup skim-milk solids	2 Tbs. butter or margarine, melted

Combine all ingredients by stirring well, and let stand for 5 minutes. Ladle about ¼ cup of batter for each pancake onto hot griddle. *Makes 12 to 16 pancakes.*

Waffles

Like pancakes, waffles can be good food as well as good fun. The recipes given here pay tribute to the complete proteins which belong in breakfast but are usually sparse or lacking. Once your family has tasted these waffles topped with fruit or, if they insist, with sauces (made with honey or molasses, as on page 19), it is improbable that they will ever again cheer the empty calories of ordinary white-flour, white-sugar waffles.

Waffle batter should not fill the baking iron completely—about half an inch from the outer edge is a good general rule. The iron should be hot enough to make a drop of water boil, but not sizzle. After you have poured the batter and closed the iron, resist the temptation to peek until the steaming has stopped.

Some cooks insist that eggs to be used in waffles must be separated and the yolks beaten and added before the stiffly beaten whites are folded in. This may make the waffles somewhat airier, but it is no crime to take a short cut and beat the whole eggs. Nutritionally speaking, the less air beaten into food the better.

Bacon or Ham Waffles

½–1 lb. bacon—or 1 cup diced ham	1 tsp. salt
2 cups unbleached or whole-wheat flour	2 tsp. brown sugar
3 tsp. baking powder	2 Tbs. wheat germ
3 Tbs. skim-milk solids	2 cups milk
	2 eggs

Fry bacon slowly until crisp. Remove from pan, drain, and crumble. Reserve ⅓ cup of the bacon fat. Combine dry ingredients and mix thoroughly to distribute well. Add milk and mix thoroughly. Beat in eggs, one at a time. Add and stir in bacon fat (⅓ cup). Pour small amount of batter on waffle iron and sprinkle with crisped bacon pieces—or diced or minced ham. (In place of bacon fat, you may use 6 tablespoons melted butter or margarine, or 3 tablespoons each of melted butter and liquid shortening.) *Makes 6 waffles.*

Cheese Waffles

2 cups unbleached or whole-wheat flour	3 eggs, beaten
1 tsp. salt	2 cups milk
3 tsp. baking powder	6 Tbs. butter or margarine, melted
3 Tbs. skim-milk solids	1 cup grated unprocessed yellow or Swiss cheese
2 Tbs. wheat germ	

Combine dry ingredients (except cheese) and mix thoroughly to distribute well. Combine and stir or beat well-beaten eggs, milk, shortening, and cheese. Add to flour mixture and stir thoroughly. *Makes 6 waffles.*

Cornmeal Waffles

1½ cups water
¾ cup undegerminated yellow cornmeal
¼ cup wheat germ
1 tsp. salt
4 Tbs. melted shortening
2 eggs, beaten
1 cup unbleached or whole-wheat flour
2 tsp. baking powder
½ tsp. baking soda
3 Tbs. skim-milk solids
(1–2 Tbs. brewers' yeast)
1⅓ cups milk

Combine cornmeal and wheat germ in top of double boiler. Pour boiling water over this mixture. Add and stir in salt and shortening. Cook for 10 minutes over boiling water, remove from heat, pour into batter bowl, and cool. When cool, add and stir in beaten eggs. Sift flour with baking powder, soda, milk solids (and brewers' yeast). Add flour mixture to bowl alternately with milk and mix thoroughly. *Makes 6 waffles.*

Oatmeal Waffles

1 cup unbleached or whole-wheat flour
½ cup oats
½ cup wheat germ
1 Tbs. brown sugar
3 tsp. baking powder
(1–2 tsp. brewers' yeast)
½ tsp. salt
2 eggs, beaten
1¼ cups milk
6 Tbs. liquid shortening

Combine all dry ingredients, mixing thoroughly. Add beaten eggs, milk, and shortening. Blend thoroughly. *Makes 6 waffles.*

Peanut Butter Waffles

¼ cup peanut butter
¼ cup wheat germ
3 Tbs. butter or margarine
2 eggs, beaten
1½ cups milk
1½ cups unbleached or whole-wheat flour
2 tsp. baking powder
3 Tbs. skim-milk solids
(1–2 Tbs. brewers' yeast)
¼ tsp. salt

Blend peanut butter, wheat germ, and butter until creamy. Add and stir beaten eggs and milk, mixing well. Sift flour with baking powder, milk solids (and brewers' yeast), and salt and add to liquid mixture. Blend thoroughly, with rotary or electric beater, until smooth. *Makes 6 waffles.*

Spice Waffles

1¼ cups unbleached or whole-wheat flour
3 tsp. baking powder
3 Tbs. skim-milk solids
1 tsp. salt
1–2 tsp. ground ginger, nutmeg, or cinnamon—or combination
1 cup wheat germ
(1 Tbs. brewers' yeast)
4 Tbs. butter or margarine, melted
2 eggs, beaten
4 Tbs. molasses
2 cups milk

Sift together flour, baking powder, milk solids, salt, and spices. Add and stir wheat germ (and brewers' yeast), distributing well. Combine and blend remaining ingredients and add liquid mixture to flour mixture. Beat until smooth. *Makes 6 waffles.*

Sweet Potato–Orange Waffles

1 cup unbleached or whole-wheat flour
2 tsp. baking powder
(1–2 Tbs. brewers' yeast)
2 Tbs. skim-milk solids
⅛ tsp. nutmeg
2–3 Tbs. wheat germ
4 Tbs. butter or margarine, melted
1 egg, beaten
1 cup milk
½ cup orange juice
1 cup mashed sweet potatoes

Sift together flour, baking powder (and brewers' yeast), milk solids, and nutmeg. Stir in wheat germ. Combine liquids with mashed sweet potatoes and blend well. Add to dry ingredients and beat until smooth. *Makes 6 waffles.*

Whole-Grain Yeast Waffles

1 package dry yeast
2 cups warm milk
2 Tbs. molasses or honey
3 eggs, beaten
6 Tbs. butter or margarine, melted
1½ cups whole-wheat or whole-buckwheat flour
½ cup wheat germ
1 tsp. salt

Stir yeast into warm milk and let stand 10 minutes. Stir in sweetener, beaten eggs, and shortening. Combine dry ingredients and stir into liquid. Mix thoroughly. Batter may be used immediately, may be allowed to rise in a warm place for 30 minutes to an hour, or may be prepared before bedtime and stored overnight in the refrigerator. *Makes 6 to 8 waffles.*

Good-Nutrition Hot Sauces for Pancakes or Waffles

Honey Sauce

1 egg yolk
½ cup milk
½ cup honey
1 Tbs. butter or
   margarine, melted

(⅛ tsp. cinnamon or
   nutmeg)

Beat egg yolk. Stir in milk, then honey. Add butter (and spice). Cook over boiling water for about 10 minutes, stirring until thickened. *Makes about 1 cup.*

Molasses Sauce

½ cup molasses
2 Tbs. butter or
   margarine
½ cup warm milk

1 Tbs. skim-milk
   solids
(⅛ tsp. ground ginger)

Heat but do not boil molasses. Stir in butter. Remove pan from heat. Combine warm milk with milk solids and slowly stir into molasses. (Add ginger.) Blend well. *Makes about 1 cup.*

Breakfast Eggs ... Plus

Eggs are fine for breakfast, supplying as they do high-quality complete proteins, an impressive list of important vitamins, and a good measure of the food minerals phosphorus, iron, and calcium. However, many people with the best of nutritional resolutions innocently believe that a breakfast egg—or, virtuously, two breakfast eggs—will provide optimum protein nutrition throughout the early part of the day. Don't misunderstand me: One or two eggs for breakfast will assuredly help stave off nutritional hypoglycemia, the low blood sugar condition so prevalent today among people of all ages, in all walks of life. But when we speak of "optimum" protein nutrition we must take into account the fact that we are aiming at an ideal—not just "adequate" or "sufficient" protein nutrition.

One egg provides the protein value of 1 ounce of meat. Even the most opportunistic of roadside stands would not insult customers by offering 1-ounce hamburgers. In order to receive the nutritive benefit of an average serving of meat, therefore, you would have to eat *three* eggs. Even this dedicated nutritionist cannot delude himself that anyone except possibly an athlete, farmer, manual laborer, or another dedicated nutritionist would willingly sit down to a three-egg breakfast as daily routine. It is a pleasant thought, but an unrealistic one; the professional nutritionist is in a position of appraising realistically the nation's eating habits by studying public health surveys and observing the traffic in physicians' offices, dental clinics, and hospitals.

Medicine and nutrition are fields of much weighty opinion, varying judgments, and sometimes arbitrary pronouncements. Many of these center about the (theoretical) roles of animal fat and cholesterol in hardening of the arteries. Despite evidence from the American Cancer Society that egg-eaters probably outlive egg-avoiders, these theories have terrified millions of people into avoiding eggs, butter, cheese, whole milk, liver and other meats, and, unbelievably, have induced pediatricians to feed babies on what is essentially an experimental diet, for which lifetime effects cannot be predicted: skimmed milk, and low fat. Actually, the majority of our cholesterol is manufactured in the body, and dietary cholesterol is a threat only to a group whose biochemical management of it is inefficient; and sugar is more of a threat (and to more people) than either fat or cholesterol. If your blood chemistry has induced your physician to taboo or limit eggs for you, remember that high quality protein is important to everyone, and can be obtained from fish, fowl, and permitted meats.

With all the disagreements, though, most nutritionists who are free of commercial pressures agree that we'd be better off if we reduced our intake of carbohydrates, particularly sugar and overprocessed starches, in favor of the whole grains; took up to 20 percent of our total fat intake from vegetable oils, with corresponding reduction of animal fats, and brought our intake of efficient (animal) proteins up to a satisfactory level. It is not easy to achieve optimal nutrition with three meals daily, and some do better with six small ones; doing it with two meals is really making life difficult.

For breakfast, meat has nutritional advantages which cannot be overemphasized. That's why so many of the recipes in preceding and succeeding pages incorporate it in pancakes, waffles, omelets.

As for the recipes to follow, I assume that you know how to boil, fry, poach, and scramble eggs. Apart from urging you to prefer poaching or short boiling to frying, to fry slowly over low heat in a minimum of fat, and to add grated yellow cheese or extra skim-milk solids to milk when scrambling eggs in little or no grease in the top of a double boiler, I shall concentrate here on only the more elaborate egg dishes representing good to excellent start-of-the-day protein nutrition.

Eggs Benedict with Cheese or Hollandaise Sauce

Traditionally served with hollandaise, which is very nice but a little tricky to make early in the morning if the original European recipe is followed, eggs benedict are also enjoyable topped with a smooth cheese dressing. In order not to horrify the purists entirely, a nonconforming recipe for hollandaise is also given.

2 English muffins*
4 slices ham
4 eggs, poached
1 cup cheese or hollandaise sauce

Break or cut muffins in half and toast them. Place a slice of ham on half a muffin, top with a poached egg, and spoon the sauce over it. *Serves 4.*

Cheese Sauce

2 Tbs. butter or margarine
2 Tbs. unbleached flour
2 Tbs. skim-milk solids
1½ cups warm milk
1 cup grated unprocessed yellow cheese
½ tsp. salt
pepper or paprika to taste

Melt butter in top of double boiler, add flour and milk solids, and blend to a smooth paste. Slowly add warm milk, stirring to avoid lumps. Add cheese and seasonings and stir until cheese melts. Cook, stirring occasionally, until sauce is smooth—about 10 minutes.

Nonconforming Hollandaise Sauce

¼ lb. butter
1–2 tsp. lemon juice
3 egg yolks, lightly beaten
1 Tbs. cream
pinch salt

Melt butter, remove pan from heat. Stir in remaining ingredients in order. Mix well, re-

A recipe for making these with whole-wheat flour is on page 64.

turn pan to very low heat, and stir constantly until sauce thickens.

Eggs Rancho

4-oz. chipped beef
1 large onion, chopped
¼ cup chopped green pepper
3 Tbs. butter, margarine, or vegetable oil
6–8 eggs
½ tsp. Worcestershire sauce
(¼ tsp. Tabasco sauce)
dash pepper or cayenne
½ cup chopped watercress or parsley
¾ cup cottage cheese

Fry chipped beef, onions, and green pepper in melted shortening, using large skillet. Stir eggs with fork until blended, season, and add to beef. Stir with fork in skillet until eggs begin to congeal; then add watercress (or parsley) and cottage cheese, stirring continuously until eggs are firm. *Serves 4.*

Eggs Corral

2 medium potatoes
8 slices bacon
1 Tbs. butter or margarine
¼ cup chopped green or sweet red pepper
¼ cup chopped onion
1 Tbs. chopped parsley or watercress
6–8 eggs
1½ cups milk
½ tsp. salt
pepper to taste

Boil potatoes in their jackets, peel, and chop. Fry bacon slowly until crisp, remove from skillet, drain, and crumble. Pour off all but 2 tablespoons of the bacon fat. Add to skillet butter, pepper, onion, and parsley (or watercress), and cook until onions brown slightly. Add chopped potatoes and mix well. Turn heat low and stir mixture occasionally to prevent burning. Stir eggs with milk in a bowl and add seasonings. Pour over potato mixture in skillet; stir to distribute all ingredients evenly and continue cooking over low heat until eggs are firm. *Serves 4.*

Eggs in Ham-Potato Nests

1½ cups mashed potatoes (white or sweet)
¼ cup wheat germ
½ cup finely diced ham
1 egg, beaten
4 eggs

Mix mashed potatoes with wheat germ, ham, and beaten egg. Shape this mixture into 4 balls and put them on a lightly greased baking sheet or in a shallow baking dish. Press centers of balls to form cups. Break an egg into each cup. Bake at 350° for 15 to 25 minutes, depending on how firm you want the eggs. *Serves 4.*

Omelets

From a nutritional standpoint, omelets are superior breakfast fare. Their special quality makes them appealing to drowsy morning appetites, and they are, besides, excellent vehicles for high-quality proteins—and not only those in the eggs themselves, but also the proteins in their fillings.

There are probably as many ways of making omelets as there are cookbooks. Some home cooks hold fast to the theory of separately beaten egg yolks and whites, some insist that perfect omelets can be made only in special omelet pans, while others try first one and then another method—fail—and give up forever in discouragement. Omelets, like soufflés, require a little self-confidence, but they are neither difficult nor fussy to make.

Individual Omelet

1 or 2 eggs	dash pepper
1 or 2 Tbs. cream	1 Tbs. butter,
¼ tsp. salt	margarine, or oil

This omelet is the easiest of all and requires no tilting. Use a 6- or 7-inch heavy skillet. Preheat slowly until very hot; then turn heat very low. Lightly beat eggs with a fork. Stir in cream, salt, and pepper. Melt butter in pan, making sure sides are coated. Pour in egg mixture and cover immediately. Let cook over lowest possible heat for 2 to 3 minutes. To remove omelet, loosen edges with spatula and turn it out on a warm plate. Fold in half.

With cheese filling: After pouring egg mixture into pan, sprinkle about ½ cup of coarsely grated unprocessed yellow cheese over it, then cover immediately. Cook 3 to 4 minutes. Cheese will be melted, egg will be done, omelet will be ready for removing, folding, and serving.

With other high-protein fillings:

Bacon: Fry 3 or 4 slices slowly until crisp. Crumble and sprinkle over omelet before folding and serving.

Ham and cottage cheese: Combine ¼ cup each of minced or deviled ham and cottage cheese and spread over omelet just before folding and serving.

Liver: ¼ pound of chicken, calf, beef, lamb, or pork liver. Chop or cut coarsely and sauté in butter or chicken fat until cooked through and just tender (a little longer for pork liver). Mix with 1 or 2 tablespoons of sour cream and spread over omelet just before folding and serving.

Kidney: ¼ pound beef, calf, lamb, or pork kidney. With scissors, remove membranes and fat. Cut into small pieces, sprinkle with 1 teaspoon of lemon juice or mild vinegar, and let stand for 20 minutes. Drain; then sauté in any shortening for 5 minutes, stirring to brown evenly. Mix with 1 or 2 tablespoons sour cream (or use leftover gravy) and spread over omelet just before folding and serving.

Larger Omelets

6–8 eggs	1 tsp. salt
¼ cup milk	dash pepper
2 Tbs. skim-milk solids	2 Tbs. butter, margarine, or oil

Use a large (12-inch), heavy skillet. Preheat slowly until very hot; then turn heat very low. Lightly beat eggs with a fork, stir in milk, milk solids, and seasonings. Melt butter in skillet, making sure sides are coated. Pour in egg mixture, cover, and cook over lowest heat for about 5 minutes. If top looks runny, lift edges with spatula, tilt pan, and let uncooked egg flow beneath cooked portion. Cover again, cook 5 minutes more. Slide onto warm plate, fold, and serve. *Serves 3 or 4.*

For filled larger omelets: Double or triple the amounts given for individual omelets.

Orange Omelet

4 eggs, lightly beaten	2 Tbs. butter,
¼ cup milk	margarine, or
½ tsp. salt	vegetable oil
¼ cup orange juice	
1 tsp. grated orange rind	

Combine all ingredients except shortening and mix thoroughly. Cook as directed for larger omelets. *Serves 2.*

3
The School Lunchbox

Good Nutrition Goes to School

Conscientious mothers who deplore the frequently pallid fare offered by many school cafeterias send their children off in the morning with judiciously packed lunchboxes. This growing habit is heartily approved by the nutritionist who sympathizes with the school dieticians' plight but would prefer to see on students' trays fewer of the ubiquitous "white specials"—creamed fish, chicken, or shreds of overdone meat; gravied mashed potatoes; macaroni or spaghetti; recipes based on white rice.

A child's lunch should supply up to a third of the day's total nutrition, depending on the size and number of his other meals, and that means up to a third of the animal proteins, minerals, and natural vitamins in food along with the carbohydrates represented by starches that are washed down, too often, with soda pop.

Youth is the ideal time to instill good nutrition habits, and it is worth the inevitable struggle with children who seem to be rebels but are actually almost total conformists.

Usually it is a fear of being different which brings about protest when the contents of the school lunchbox resemble real food instead of blackmail payments in the form of white-bread sandwiches, sugary cookies, and candy bars. As one youngster complained to his newly nutrition-conscious mother, "I'm the only one in my whole class who brings crazy-looking bread to school. Besides, all the other fellows get candy for dessert, and you expect me to eat this darned old banana or apple every day. They think I'm a square."

The child's mother patiently pointed out that he was also the only one in his class to go without a cold lately, and that most of the other fellows spent their Saturday mornings in a dentist's chair. Needless to say, the hero of this story was not impressed, preferring the anonymities of tribal resemblance (sniffles and cavities) to the dubious distinction of being uniquely healthy.

The school lunchbox need not contain crazy-looking food to be healthful, but neither need it be patterned after nutritional nonentities. Even that good old stand-by symbolizing youth's solidarity—the peanut butter sandwich—can be made eminently (and undetectably) nutritious (page 24).

It does seem a shame, however, that mothers must connive in order to provide their young with proper nutrition. Actually, changing youthful eating habits is less of a losing game than one would suspect, although of course starting from scratch is easier—and preferable. Children brought up from infancy on superior foods prefer whole-grain cereals and breads to sugary sawdust crackles and too-soft, too-white, too-tasteless breads. They even prefer fruits to candies, and milk or fruit juices to soda pop.

When good nutrition enters the child's home late in his life, it is still possible to guide him away from sweets based on sugar by offering similar toothsome fare in sugarless or sugar-minimum forms. It is only in the most adamantly nutrition-insistent homes that ordinary breakfast cereals, wax-wrapped white breads, cakes, cookies, pies, and other "normal" staples of American diet are absent. As wisdom in the ways of good health through nutrition filters through to homemakers, the unfortunate tendency is to go all-out faddish in an extreme of zealous concern. This cannot help but make nutrition a nasty nine-letter word, especially to husbands and children. They must eat the new order of meals in this matriarchal society, but they seldom do it in gracious silence.

"Something Hot"

It is always nice for each meal to contain a hot dish. Remember, however, that a cold dish or meal with superior nutrients in it is far preferable to one whose chief claim to virtue lies in the fact that it's hot.

Rather than rely on school cafeteria steam tables, it may be a good idea to equip the child's lunchbox with a wide-mouthed thermos in which a variety of hot foods can be carried to school. There's always soup, and most children like it—especially if they can enjoy the home-forbidden delight of "drinking" it instead of spooning it up like little ladies or gentlemen, neither of which most of them care to be.

If you cook soup by the can-opener method, you can fortify it in a number of ways. Heat cream-style soups as directed with a can of whole milk, but add two or three tablespoons of skim-milk solids for extra protein and calcium. Canned tomato soup, diluted with milk and milk solids, is delicious with an added tablespoonful of yeast flakes per cup. Good canned vegetable, beef, or chicken soup becomes better if you add chunks of leftover cooked meat or chicken. All soups can be accompanied by whole-wheat, whole-rye, or wheat-germ crackers to be dunked.

The wide-mouthed thermos can also contain nutritious versions of fish chowders, macaroni* and cheese, spaghetti* and meatballs, Spanish rice,* stews, and casseroles.

Indignant school cafeteria dieticians may point out that their steam tables destroy no more nutrients than are lost because of the length of time home-prepared foods remain in the thermos before being consumed. There is a certain justice in this, except that you can pack much more nutrition in a hot dish than is usually found at school. Be generous with the use of skim-milk solids, wheat germ, brewers' yeast, and yeast flakes—sources of vitamins and proteins greatly needed by growing bodies.

Keep Lunchboxes Green!

Children who ordinarily scorn the dinner salad course may take more kindly to salad ingredients packed in lunchboxes. They can be eaten with the fingers without parental admonishment. Taken crisp from the refrigerator and tucked in a plastic bag, a few leaves of lettuce, celery stalks (filled with soft cheese, perhaps), radishes, carrot curls, green or red pepper rings, and whole small tomatoes may find their way into young stomachs at lunchtime after serving a useful purpose as targets, guns, darts, or Indian headdresses.

The Inevitable Sandwich

Sandwiches can and should provide excellent nutrition. If the children object to whole-wheat bread exclusively, take a hint from fancy tearooms which offer sandwich plates of bite-size sandwiches made with a variety of breads. If little sandwiches are too dainty for your youngsters or take too much trouble to prepare, at least vary the lunchbox sandwich bread by using more than one kind, or making triple-deckers with at least one slice of whole-wheat. Bake your own white bread (see page 65) or look for a commercial white bread made from unbleached flour, wheat germ, soy, nonfat milk, and other nutritious ingredients. For reducers: double the protein content of the

---

Macaroni and spaghetti made with wheat germ and supplying 20 percent protein are commercially available. Rice should be brown or converted.

sandwich, omit the top piece of bread, and wrap tightly in foil.

One sure way to get a child to accept whole-grain bread is to make it yourself. Even after it has been wrapped in waxed paper or sandwich bags, there's something about the smell of home-baked bread that is irresistible. Its taste is so much more delicious that once they've been exposed to it children grow dissatisfied with pasty and gummy white breads and accept more readily the commercial whole-wheat varieties which have a firmer texture and a breadier smell.

Sandwich Fillings

Peanut Butter
If you own an electric blender, you can make your own peanut butter and be absolutely certain of its chemical purity as well as its content of unhydrogenated (unsaturated) fat. Put shelled peanuts in the blender a handful at a time and let them agitate at low speed until they are powdery. Either start with salted peanuts or add salt before the next step. (The little red-skin Spanish peanuts contain more nutrients than the big naked kind. Use skins and all.) Pour the pulverized peanuts in a jar or bowl and mix with peanut oil or any other vegetable oil until the desired consistency is reached. (Up to one-fourth of the oil can be wheat-germ oil if a jar of peanut butter disappears in your house within two weeks.)

This homemade peanut butter may separate, unlike the homogenized kind bought in stores. A good trick is to stand the jar upside down on the shelf, where the oil will rise to the *bottom*. The other alternative is to stir it up before each use. A bit more trouble—but a bit more nutritious, too.

Whether you use store-bought or homemade peanut butter, you can make it doubly nutritious if you mix it with equal parts of wheat germ. The kids don't have to know you've monkeyed with it. Simply save your last empty jar of a favorite chunk-style brand. Fill it and an empty new jar with the double amount of peanut butter yielded when you extend it with an equal quantity of wheat germ. When your young critic mentions that this batch tastes swell (you might) tell him your secret. I suggest this not only because I believe in being as truthful with a child as you hope him to be, but also because he may subsequently, with your

encouragement, decide to add wheat germ to breakfast cereals and other foods.

For the school lunchbox or the after-school snack, a peanut butter sandwich can furnish additional food value if it contains bits of crumbled crisp bacon and even more if it also includes a slice of unprocessed yellow cheese.

Other Sandwich Filling Suggestions
chopped hot dogs with pickle relish and mustard or chili sauce

chopped chicken or turkey with minced celery, parsley, and mayonnaise

ground or minced ham with grated yellow cheese, chopped hard-cooked egg, and mayonnaise

tuna fish or salmon with chopped green peppers and celery

boneless sardines mashed with hard-cooked egg and lemon juice

chopped yellow cheese with crisp bacon

sliced meat loaf with chopped pimientos

minced shrimp, lobster, or crab meat with cream cheese

cottage cheese with chopped raw vegetables

chopped cooked liver with hard-cooked egg yolk and mayonnaise

sliced roast beef, lamb, pork, or veal with sliced tomato

sliced tongue with mustard, pickle, and slivered yellow cheese

liverwurst, salami, or bologna with cole slaw

Sweet Sandwiches
cottage cheese and honey or dark molasses

cream cheese, minced ham, and crushed pineapple

any soft cheese mixed with chopped nuts and dark molasses

cream cheese with chopped cashew nuts and chopped crystallized ginger

cottage cheese with grated orange rind

grated carrots and raisins moistened with honey

cottage cheese mixed with skim-milk solids and wheat germ, moistened with cream, and sweetened with honey or dark molasses

Lunchbox Desserts

With a hot dish and/or a sandwich or two, the school lunchbox is only indifferently filled, according to the children who are going to eat its contents. What they are looking for is a special treat. Fruit, they may admit grudgingly, is all right once in a while—especially bananas. But for Pete's sake, can't they have cookies and cake like the other kids? On the playground stock market, fruit is sold short in active trading. If you want to make financiers out of your youngsters, you'll give them something that commands a high price in a bullish market. The result will most likely be that they'll reserve their attractive holdings for themselves.

Good nutrition, let it be repeated, need not—should not—be dull. Perfectly nutritious cakes and cookies are possible, but you'll probably have to make them yourself. If you're really serious about this business of giving your children a better start in life by feeding them nothing but the best in nutrition, please look in the index for cake and cookie recipes.

Lunchbox Beverages

Don't fill the narrow-mouthed thermos bottle with milk. The children can usually buy a container at lunchtime, and they drink plenty of it at home. Fill the thermos with fruit juice instead—fresh or frozen—and vary the juices from day to day.

The strategy here is not only to get extra vitamin C into growing bodies which need it, but also to cut down on the consumption of bottled sodas. The hard work of study or play causes thirst, as any youngster with a bottle in his hand will remind you. (To this observer, it would appear that the soda pop bottle has become a modern biological mutation, permanently attached to a small hand.) Don't make the mistake of telling your child that sweet sodas only make them thirstier, whereas fruit juices truly quench thirst. It happens to be true, but juvenile reasoning and logic are not the same. Tell them, instead, that fruit juices will make them stronger and better outfielders or skaters, if boys, or prettier and better outfielders or skaters, if girls. In any case—if you are driven to an extremity, become a Stern Parent. Cola beverages are so acid that skilled laboratory workers can identify, by tooth erosion, a rat given one single drink of these concoctions. Their caffeine content is high enough to make the parent who allows these and forbids coffee, at very least, inconsistent. The others contain artificial colors and flavors of dubious safety, and they supply five teaspoonfuls of sugar per bottle, which at best is a contribution to weight problems, and at worst a pathway to diabetes, hypoglycemia, hardening of the arteries, and heart disease. If you get the familiar argument that Johnny's mother lets him drink them, respond with: "Some mothers let their children ride bicycles in heavy traffic, but that doesn't mean we must, or that it's a safe thing to do."

Last thought on beverages: the "natural" sugars of fruit juices are also mischief-makers, but at least are accompanied by body-building substances missing from the sodas, and don't contain food additives. Even these should not be overdone: the Greeks did have a word for it, and it makes nutritional sense—*moderation.*

4
Salads and
Salad Dressings

What Is a Salad?

From a good-nutrition standpoint, every meal except breakfast should either include a salad or begin with one. The author does not, however, believe that all of the dressing-drenched, fancied-up concoctions of meat, fish, fowl, cooked vegetables, or macaroni products deserve to be called "salads." In my nutrition lexicon, a salad is composed of raw green leaves—any number, variety, or combination of green leaves (and there are a couple of dozen of them)—with or without other raw vegetables.

These ingredients should be as fresh as possible, kept under refrigeration until prepared, washed briefly under running cold water, dried quickly, and refrigerated again until served. Just before serving they should be tossed lightly with a small amount of dressing.

To list the greens and raw vegetables suitable for salads would be a waste of space, because such a list would include practically every vegetable that grows above or below the ground. Almost any vegetable that can be eaten cooked can be eaten raw. There are a few exceptions, of course. Your common sense will tell you that mushrooms, for example, should be cooked a little before eating, but only because that's how their flavor is best. Even such vegetables as eggplant, beets, turnips, squash, asparagus, and white or sweet potatoes can be added profitably to salads if they are grated, diced, shoestringed, or sliced thinly. Garden-fresh corn kernels are delicious raw if picked while still young, before the cobs toughen.

No formal recipes for salads as such are given in this book. Any other cookbook in print will give you from twenty to fifty pages or more of vegetable names and how to combine them. As far as I'm concerned, they are all good. In any mixture, any raw vegetable salad represents the good nutrition advocated in these pages. I'd like to think you'll eat more of them, more often than you do now.

As for salad dressings, the supermarket shelves are loaded with good ones of all flavors and varying caloric content. Unless you prefer to make your own (pages 27–28) they are perfectly all right to use—always in moderation. Dressings are supposed to enhance the flavor of salad ingredients, not drown it.

Special Note: The nutritive contribution of both commercial and homemade salad dressings can be raised tremendously by the addition of small amounts of wheat-germ oil, which is a concentrated powerhouse of B-complex vitamins, vitamin E, unsaturated fatty acids, phosphatides, and other nutrients.

How to Use Wheat-Germ Oil in Salad Dressings

In commercial dressings: Begin by adding 1 teaspoonful to an 8-ounce bottle. When you have used some of the dressing in the bottle, add another teaspoonful. When you discover that this remarkable nutrient has not changed the taste of your salad dressing, which is consumed without comment by your family, use it in increasingly greater amounts—up to 2 tablespoons per 8-ounce bottle.

In homemade dressings: Begin by using 1 teaspoonful to replace 1 teaspoonful of oil, gradually increasing the amount until, in subsequent usages, you are replacing one-fourth of the oil with wheat-germ oil.

Fruit salads? They're fine—when made of fresh fruit in any combination and served as a dessert course, at lunch, or between meals. Generally speaking, you would do better to eat fruits in the hand rather than fussing as much as you must when making a salad of them. The less air, heat, light, and time they are exposed to when their skins are broken, the better.

Other popular "salads"—chicken, seafood, cold cuts, etc.—are fine also when served as the main course of a light meal. They do not represent the superb nutritional equilibrium provided by a raw leaf and vegetable salad eaten in conjunction with a dinner's content of meat, cooked vegetables, and carbohydrates.

Basic Low-Calorie Salad Dressings

No. 1. Vinegar Dressing

½ cup mild vinegar
¼ cup water
1 clove garlic, minced
½ tsp. salt
¼ tsp. paprika
½ tsp. liquid sugar substitute
1 Tbs. chopped fresh parsley or chives

Combine all ingredients in a bottle. Shake and chill. *Makes ⅔ cup.*

No. 2 Citrus-Herb Dressing

½ tsp. unflavored gelatin
1 Tbs. water
½ cup boiling water
½ tsp. liquid sugar substitute—or 1 Tbs. brown sugar
½ tsp. salt
⅔ cup lemon juice
¼ tsp. onion juice or powder
⅛ tsp. garlic powder
⅛ tsp. curry powder
⅛ tsp. paprika

Moisten gelatin with cold water, then dissolve in boiling water. Add sweetener and salt. When thoroughly dissolved, remove from heat and cool. Combine in a bottle with all other ingredients, shake well, and chill. *Makes 1 cup.*

No. 3. Cream-Style Dressing

½ cup plain yogurt or buttermilk
½ cup skim milk
1 Tbs. white vinegar
¼ tsp. salt
⅛ tsp. white pepper
¼ tsp. dry mustard
dash each of garlic and onion salt

Combine all ingredients in a bottle, shake, and chill. *Makes 1 cup.*

Other Good-Nutrition Salad Dressings

French Dressing

1 Tbs. wheat-germ oil
5 Tbs. olive, peanut, or salad oil
2 Tbs. lemon juice —or 1 each of lemon juice and vinegar
1 tsp. brown sugar
¼ tsp. salt
¼ tsp. paprika
1 clove garlic

Combine all ingredients except garlic in a bowl or electric blender. Mix vigorously with rotary or electric beater until thoroughly blended. Pour into jar or bottle and add garlic. Refrigerate, and shake before each using. If this amount has not been consumed within a week, remove the garlic. *Makes ½ cup.*

To vary this dressing, as you enjoy more and more salads, add one of the following from time to time to ½ cup, just before serving. Shake well:

¼ tsp. basil, oregano, tarragon, dry mustard, chili powder, or mixed herbs
2–4 Tbs. Roquefort or bleu cheese
¼ cup chopped onion
2 Tbs. catsup or chili sauce
1 Tbs. horseradish
1 Tbs. each of chopped anchovies and capers
2 Tbs. chopped fresh parsley, mint, or watercress
¼ cup sweet or sour cream (beat in slowly)

Mayonnaise

2 egg yolks
½ tsp. salt
¼ tsp. paprika
⅛ tsp. dry mustard
3 Tbs. lemon juice
1 Tbs. vinegar
2 Tbs. wheat-germ oil
¾ cup olive, peanut, or salad oil

Chill bowl and all ingredients except seasonings in refrigerator before starting. Using either a wire whisk or your electric mixer or blender, beat egg yolks thoroughly. Add and beat in dry ingredients until well blended; then add alternately—and slowly—the lemon juice, vinegar, and oils. If mayonnaise shows a tendency to separate or curdle, beat another chilled egg yolk in a cold bowl and slowly stir into this the mayonnaise. This will solve the problem—and provide still better nutrition. If the dressing seems too thick, stir in enough sweet or sour cream to thin it to the desired consistency. *Makes 1 large cup.*

Thousand Island Dressing

To ½ cup mayonnaise, add:

2 Tbs. chili sauce
1 Tbs. catsup
1 Tbs. chopped pickles
   or olives
1 tsp. minced onion

1 tsp. each of chopped
   green pepper and
   pimiento
yolk of hard-cooked
   egg, grated

Russian Dressing

To ½ cup mayonnaise, add:

1–2 Tbs. chopped
   pimiento, green
   pepper, or pepper
   relish

¼ cup chili sauce
1 tsp. Worcestershire
   sauce

Sour Cream Dressing

¾ cup sour cream
¼ cup skim-milk
   solids
½ tsp. minced onion
   or onion juice
(pressed juice of ¼
   clove garlic)
1 Tbs. chopped
   parsley, watercress,
   or chives

¼ tsp. celery salt
¼ tsp. salt
dash pepper, paprika,
   or cayenne
2–3 Tbs. lemon juice
   or vinegar

Beat sour cream until smooth and add all other ingredients in order—lemon juice or vinegar last—beat until creamy. *Makes 1 large cup.*

5
Beautiful Soup

Soup is art and philosophy combined, reflecting the ingenuity, creativity, and thought processes of the one who prepares it.

Anyone with a minimum of manual dexterity is able to open a can, and what's inside is frequently satisfying and tasty. Canned soups are also, as their advertisers proclaim, "nourishing." They contain calories and varying amounts of proteins, minerals, vitamins, fats, and carbohydrates. No one can deny it. No one can deny either that soup unadorned out of a can tastes like canned soup, or that soup made by the vatful lacks the aroma, grace, and reassurance of love which emanate from a steaming pot on the back of Mother's range.

Gourmet and psychological considerations aside, there is much to be said nutritionally in favor of homemade soup—even if the "home" part of this consists only in fortifying and glorifying the 10 ounces of densely concentrated base that slurps out of a can. The chances are your vegetables won't be any fresher than those used by the cannery—but they'll be cooked more briefly and they'll be consumed sooner. The meat, fowl, or fish you use will be present in more generous quantities. And if you are conscientious, the water you use for homemade soup will not be plain H_2O, but the repository of nutrients from vegetables you have cooked for other purposes. If you have the time and the will, you'll extract the best part of bones—their calcium and proteins—by cracking them before adding them to the soup pot. You'll also save vegetable parings, outer leaves, meat scraps, and cooked leftovers of all kinds to contribute their otherwise wasted food value. Like America itself, the soup vessel is a melting pot—and one that can contribute greatly to good nutrition.

Granted, you must be soup-minded in order to see beauty in the ragged end of a roast, the leaves and peelings of vegetables, the uneaten bowl of oatmeal, the skin and bones of broiled or roasted chicken, the clean, meaty bone a kind neighbor or butcher donates to your dog (through you as intermediary). But here's a little secret: If you privately yearn to achieve the reputation of being a fabulous cook, you can sail toward your goal on every plateful of homemade soup you put before your family or guests. All the bits and scraps you toss into the soup pot along with water saved from last night's—or last week's— vegetables have a way of blending together like a fine orchestration. It requires only for you to taste, sip, criticize, and correct.

Soup Stocks

Economy Stock From
Bones, Raw Meat Scraps, Etc.

Crack bones, if they are large. Brown them and the meat scraps in a small amount of their own fat or oil, or other shortening. Remove from pan and pour off melted fat. Put bones and browned scraps in bottom of heavy pot and pour over them enough water to cover to twice their depth. Bring to a brisk boil, cover pot, lower heat, and simmer for 3 or 4 hours. Decant liquid and allow it to cool. Fat will rise to the top and can be removed easily. Return stock to clean pot and enrich further by adding whatever vegetable parings or top leaves you have, along with cooked table scraps. Bring to a boil again and simmer for 30 minutes. Strain, cool, and again remove fat if any has accumulated.

You now have an economical, perfectly good stock suitable as a base for all kinds of soups or gravies or as a more nutritious liquid than plain water for stews and pot roasts. Seasonings are not added to this basic stock, for the use to which you put it later will determine the seasonings. Store in freezer or refrigerator.

Economy Poultry Stock

An excellent chicken-flavored stock can be made with the raw feet, necks, hearts, and gizzards, plus discarded cooked skin and bones without sacrificing the bird itself, which you may prefer fried, broiled, or roasted.

Cover poultry feet with boiling water and boil for 5 minutes. Discard water and remove skin, being careful not to throw away the jellylike substance between the small bones. Cut or break the bones into smaller pieces and add them to a pot containing the hearts, gizzards, and cooked skin and bones. Cover these with (vegetable) water to twice their depth and bring to a brisk boil. Lower heat and simmer, covered, for 2 hours.

Without interrupting boil, at end of 2 hours add tops and outer stalks of celery, along with a few outer leaves of lettuce, and, if you have them, carrots, peas, white turnips, parsnips, squash—alone or in combination—a total of ½ cup. Boil for 30 minutes more. Strain. Discard bones, but if you have pets by all means give them the skin, gizzards, hearts, and vegetables. When broth is cool, remove fat and store in freezer or refrigerator.

Economy Vegetable Stock

Good cooks with an eye on nutritional values can have constantly on hand a fine supply of vitamin-rich vegetable stock for use in gravies, pot roasts, stews, and casseroles, as well as soup—and, odd as this may seem to you, for use in baking also.

All you have to do is save (under refrigeration, please) a week's supply of the vegetable parts ordinarily and profligately thrown away —peelings, tops, unused stalks, roots, and shoots. Keep a large polyethylene bag in the refrigerator to receive these valuable discards. Also, keep a 2-quart jar on the top shelf and pour into this the *small* amount of water you use when you cook vegetables for the table. When the jar is full, you should have collected enough solid material to make a batch of stock.

Wash the vegetable discards and pick them over for obvious defects. Chop them, or put them through the coarse blade of your meat grinder. To each 2 cups or more of chopped vegetables, add 2 quarts of vegetable water. Bring to a boil, lower the heat, and simmer for ½ hour or longer. If you must have fairly clear stock, remove the vegetables. Nutrition is best served by putting everything through a food mill or forcing it through a sieve. This yields a purée. For thinner liquids, add more vegetable water.

Needless to say, it's up to you to use some discretion in the choice of vegetable discards and/or water which go into the stock. If you use overlarge quantities of "strong" vegetables like onions, cabbage, broccoli, and turnips, the stock will be strong. Carrots, parsnips, and the pods of green peas tend to sweeten the stock. A judicious combination of many different-flavored vegetables will blend deliciously, no one predominating—unless you want it to.

Economy Mushroom Stock

Save the stems, peelings, and broken pieces when you prepare mushrooms as a side vegetable or to use in recipes. Wash quickly in a sieve or colander under running water.

Sauté these mushroom remnants in a little butter—just enough to prevent sticking—and stir them just long enough to coat them (about 2 minutes). To each cupful of mushroom pieces add 2 cups of vegetable water. Bring to a boil, lower heat, and simmer for 5 to 10 minutes. This may be used as is, or you may strain it and use only the liquid if you have any qualms about eating the peelings—which you shouldn't have.

Rich Beef Stock

2 lbs. lean beef plus bones	1½ cups chopped mixed raw vegetables
2 tsp. salt	
2 qts. (vegetable) water	½ cup tomatoes

Cut about a third of the beef into small pieces and crack as many of the bones as you can. Brown these quickly in a little beef fat. Put the browned beef and bones and the rest of the raw beef and bones in a large kettle, salt them, cover, and let stand for 1 hour. Add the (vegetable) water, bring to a boil, lower heat, and simmer for 3 hours.

Do not, unless you absolutely insist on clear stock, remove the scum which bubbles to the top. It is rich in nutrients.

At the end of 3 hours add the vegetables and simmer for another ½ hour. Pick out the pieces of lean meat; then strain the stock and let it cool. When cold, remove all but a little of the fat which has risen to the top. The stock is a ready-made soup after you have tasted it and corrected the seasoning. It can be stored as a rich beef stock for use as the base of other soups or for adding proteins to meatless casseroles.

As for the meat and vegetables, they have lost most of their prime nutritive value after such long cooking, but they still have some virtue. Meat can be shredded and added to heavy soups like minestrone, gumbo, bean, or split pea. It can be minced and mixed with the yolk of a raw egg and wheat germ as a sandwich filling. It can be used with raw chopped meat for stuffed peppers and similar recipes, or in spaghetti sauce. As a last resort, mix it in with your pet's food along with the vegetables.

Chicken Stock No. 1

Stewing fowl, about 5 lbs.	1 cup celery leaves
	¼ cup chopped carrots
3 qts. (vegetable) water	½ medium onion
1 cup chopped celery stalks	1 tsp. salt

Cut fowl into pieces, add water, cover, bring to a boil, lower heat, and simmer for 2 hours. Add vegetables and salt and simmer for ½ hour longer. Cool and remove fat. If soup has jellied, heat it until it is liquid again and strain. (Use the cooked chicken, of course, for fricassee, salad, à la king, or sandwiches.)

Chicken Stock No. 2

2–3 lbs. of chicken backs, wings, and necks	1½ cups chopped mixed vegetables, including leaves of celery or lettuce, and onion
2 qts. (vegetable) water	
1 tsp. salt	

Proceed as for Chicken Stock No. 1. The meat can be carefully separated from the bones and used in croquettes, soufflés, sandwiches, or pancake fillings.

Good-Nutrition Soups

Arthur's Potato and Swiss Cheese Soup

4 medium potatoes	salt and pepper to taste
1 large onion	
4 Tbs. butter or margarine	dash nutmeg
	4–8 Tbs. grated Swiss cheese
1 Tbs. unbleached or whole-wheat flour	4 tsp. finely chopped parsley
½ cup warm milk	
1 qt. boiling stock, mild vegetable water, or (in a pinch) plain water, to which add 2 or 3 bouillon cubes	

Peel and dice potatoes and onion, and brown lightly in 2 tablespoons of butter or margarine. Melt remaining 2 tablespoons of butter or margarine in a heavy soup kettle and add flour, stirring to a smooth paste. Stir in ½ cup of warm milk slowly to avoid lumps. Add boiling stock (or water) and browned potato-onion mixture and stir thoroughly. Season to taste. Simmer gently until potatoes are tender. Add dash of nutmeg, stir again, and pour over grated cheese in soup plates (1 or 2 tablespoons per plate, depending on how much you like cheese). Sprinkle with parsley. *Serves 4.*

Vegetable-Cheese Soup

3 Tbs. butter, margarine, or peanut oil	3 Tbs. whole-wheat or unbleached flour
	3 Tbs. water
½ cup thinly sliced or diced carrots	1 qt. milk
	½ cup skim-milk solids
½ cup thinly sliced green celery	
1 cup cut green beans	1–2 cups grated unprocessed yellow cheese
2 cups boiling stock or (vegetable) water	

Heat butter, margarine or peanut oil in heavy soup kettle. Cook vegetables until they are well coated—about 5 minutes. Add boiling stock (or water), cover kettle, and simmer over low heat until vegetables are tender but not soft—about 10 minutes. Make a smooth paste of the flour and water and add slowly to the kettle. Simmer, stirring, until soup thickens slightly—about 3 minutes. Combine milk and milk solids and add to kettle. Add cheese and stir over low heat until cheese melts and blends. Do not boil. *Serves 8.*

Borsch

4 or 5 medium beets	1 cup tomato purée or
2 or 3 large carrots	stewed tomatoes
1 small head green	1 Tbs. lemon juice
cabbage	salt and pepper to
2 medium onions,	taste
chopped	(1 Tbs. brewers' yeast)
1 stalk celery with	sour cream
leaves, chopped	(optional: 4–6 Tbs. dry
2 Tbs. butter or	red wine)
margarine	
1 qt. stock or	
(vegetable) water	

Scrub well but do not peel beets and carrots. Shred them and the cabbage fairly fine. Melt butter or margarine in heavy soup kettle and sauté onions and celery until well coated but not brown—3 to 4 minutes. Add stock or vegetable water, tomatoes, and lemon juice and bring to a boil. Add shredded vegetables and simmer 10 to 15 minutes. Season to taste (and add brewers' yeast) and stir. Ladle into bowls or soup plates. (Stir in 1 tablespoon dry red wine per adult serving.) Serve with side dishes or bowl of sour cream for topping. *Serves 4 to 6.*

Fresh Pea Pod Soup

2 lbs. fresh young	2 Tbs. skim-milk
peas in pods	solids
1 bay leaf	¼ cup milk or light
2 qts. (vegetable)	cream
water	salt and pepper to
(1 ham bone or lean	taste
end of tongue, if	3–4 Tbs. yeast flakes
you have it)	

Wash peas in their pods, shuck them, and, reserving the peas, put pods only in soup kettle with bay leaf and water (and ham bone or tongue). Bring to a boil, lower heat, and sim-

mer for 1 hour. Drain, saving the broth and discarding the pods, bay leaf, ham, or tongue. Cover reserved peas with pod broth and boil very gently for 10 to 12 minutes until peas are soft. Force through food mill or sieve, or purée in electric blender. Return purée to kettle. Combine milk solids with milk or cream and stir into purée. Add seasonings and yeast flakes and heat, but do not allow to boil. *Serves 6 to 8.*

Onion Soup

Of course you can tear open an envelope of dehydrated soup mix, add water, bring to a boil, and serve a creditable onion soup. But fine French onion soup is not difficult to prepare, so why not treat the family or guests occasionally and bask in their admiration? Besides, you'll be serving more excellent onion nutrients at one sitting than you probably do in any average week.

1 lb. onions, sliced	salt and pepper to
very thin	taste
2 Tbs. butter	(2–4 Tbs. yeast
2 Tbs. whole-wheat or	flakes)
unbleached flour	6–8 slices crusty
6–8 cups stock—or	French bread
vegetable water,	grated Parmesan
adding ½ bouillon	cheese
cube per cup	(6–8 Tbs. sherry)

Sauté thinly sliced onions in butter, using heavy saucepan and stirring to coat well. Avoid excessive browning. When onions are glazed and golden in color, sprinkle flour over them, stir, and cook for 1 minute. Add stock slowly, stirring constantly. When smooth and well blended, add seasonings. If you have time, remove the pan from heat and allow it to stand for an hour or more. Bring slowly to serving temperature (add yeast flakes at this time) while you sprinkle slices of French bread with Parmesan cheese and toast them in the oven until the cheese melts and browns. Ladle soup into bowls or plates. (A tablespoonful of sherry per serving is delicious—for adults.) Float a piece of toast in each; pass more Parmesan cheese for the gourmets. *Serves 6 to 8.*

Vegetable Soup

The vegetables called for in this recipe are not fixed by law. You can vary them in any way you see fit, provided you maintain approximately the same proportion of vegetables to liquid. Green beans, yellow beans, lima beans, turnips, parsnips, chopped spinach or cabbage, shredded outer leaves of lettuce, etc.—are all excellent soup material. Use what you have on hand or choose vegetables in season.

2 Tbs. butter
½ cup thinly sliced celery, with leaves
¼ cup chopped onion
1 cup diced carrots
2 cups diced potatoes
1 cup fresh, frozen, or canned peas
4 tomatoes, coarsely cut, or 1 can whole or stewed tomatoes

1 or 2 green peppers, chopped
1 Tbs. chopped parsley
1 bay leaf
salt and pepper to taste
(2 Tbs. brewers' yeast or yeast flakes)
2 qts. stock or vegetable water

Melt butter and sauté celery and onions for 2 or 3 minutes. Add these along with all other vegetables and seasonings (and yeast) to stock in soup kettle. Bring to boil, lower heat, and cook for about 30 minutes. Remove bay leaf before serving. *Serves 6 to 8.*

Beet-Top Soup

You can use spinach instead, but beet tops are higher in nutritive value and are often discarded when fresh beets are served—a phenomenon absolutely incomprehensible to a nutritionist.

3 Tbs. butter
1 medium onion, finely chopped
2 lbs. beet tops, coarsely chopped

4 cups stock or vegetable water
salt and pepper to taste

Melt butter and cook onion over low heat until golden but not brown. Add beet tops and stir them around with a fork to coat them. Add stock and seasonings, stir, and simmer until greens are tender. *Serves 4 to 6.*

Italian Spinach Soup

If you have beet tops, combine them with the spinach to yield the amount called for.

2 qts. boiling stock or vegetable water
½ cup chopped onion
1 Tbs. chopped parsley
½ cup thinly sliced celery

4 coarsely cut tomatoes—or 1 can whole Italian tomatoes
½ cup diced carrots
2 cups cooked chopped spinach

2 Tbs. olive oil
2 cups cooked brown rice

salt and pepper to taste
grated Parmesan cheese

Add to boiling stock the onion, parsley, celery, tomatoes, and carrots and simmer until celery is just tender—about 12 to 18 minutes. Sauté spinach in olive oil, stirring to coat well—about 2 minutes. Stir into simmering stock, add rice and seasonings, and cook for 5 minutes. Serve with grated Parmesan cheese. *Serves 6 to 8.*

Liver Soup

½ lb. beef, pork, or lamb liver
4 cups boiling stock, vegetable water, or bouillon made with cubes
3 Tbs. butter or margarine
1 cup chopped mushrooms

1 Tbs. chopped parsley
1 tsp. salt
⅛ tsp. paprika
1 Tbs. whole-wheat flour
1 cup milk
2 Tbs. skim-milk solids

Drop liver into boiling stock for 2 minutes. Remove liver (reserving stock) and grind or chop fine. Sauté ground liver for 2 minutes in 2 tablespoons of the butter, stirring. Add mushrooms and sauté for 2 minutes more. Transfer to stock pot, add parsley and seasonings, and simmer, covered, for 20 minutes. Melt remaining tablespoon of butter, add flour, and blend to a smooth paste. Add a little of the soup and stir until very smooth; then pour back into the soup and stir. Bring to a boil, lower heat, add milk and milk solids, and stir over very low heat for 5 minutes. Do not boil. *Serves 6 to 8.*

Oxtail Soup

2 lbs. oxtail, disjointed
3–4 Tbs. whole-wheat or unbleached flour
2 Tbs. cooking oil
8 cups vegetable water
1½ tsp. salt
⅛ tsp. black pepper
1 small bay leaf
1 Tbs. chopped parsley

½ cup chopped onion
½ cup diced carrots
½ cup chopped celery
(½ cup diced turnips or parsnips)
¼ tsp. thyme
¼ tsp. basil or oregano
1 tsp. Worcestershire sauce
(sherry, if desired)

Trim excess fat from oxtail joints. Dredge joints in flour and brown (in heavy soup kettle) on all sides in oil. Add vegetable water, salt, pepper, bay leaf, and parsley. Bring to boil and boil briskly for 10 minutes. Skim soup, discard bay leaf, cover kettle, lower heat, and simmer for 3 hours. Remove oxtails, separate meat from bones, and set aside. Add to kettle the chopped vegetables and herbs and simmer until vegetables are soft—about 20 minutes. Force through food mill or sieve and return to kettle. Add the reserved bits of oxtail meat and heat to serving temperature. Before serving, stir in Worcestershire sauce. Or, omit this, ladle soup into bowls or plates, and stir in up to 1 tablespoon sherry per adult serving. *Serves 6 to 8.*

Mushroom and Barley Soup

You can be old-fashioned and old-world about this and use barley, which, like all grains used in this cook book, should be whole grain; or you can be modern and new-world by substituting brown rice for the barley.

½ cup barley or brown rice	4 cups seasoned beef stock
3 cups vegetable water or bouillon made with cubes	½ cup diced carrots ½ cup diced celery (1–2 Tbs. brewers' yeast or yeast flakes)
½ tsp. salt	
½ lb. mushrooms	
2 Tbs. butter	

Let cold tap water run over barley or rice in a strainer; then add it slowly to boiling vegetable water and season with salt. Stir, cover, then simmer over low heat until cereal is soft and water is absorbed. Stir occasionally to prevent sticking or scorching. Sauté mushrooms in butter for 2 minutes; then add them to boiling stock along with the barley or rice. Mix thoroughly, lower heat, and simmer for 20 minutes. Add carrots and celery and simmer for 20 minutes more, until vegetables are tender. The soup should then be thick enough. If you prefer it thicker, remove a few tablespoons of the barley or rice and force through a food mill or sieve, returning it to the soup. (Stir in brewers' yeast or yeast flakes before serving.) *Serves 4 to 6.*

Fish Chowders

Some of the best nutrition in the world comes to us from the depths of oceans and lakes or the shallows of streams. Not only are fish high in first-rate proteins, vitamins, and minerals, but they also have another advantage peculiar to the times we live in. Nobody sprays the waterways with DDT or fertilizes them with poisonous chemicals.

Salmon or Tuna Fish Chowder

⅓ cup diced salt pork	1 flat can red salmon or tuna fish
1 onion, finely chopped	1⅔ cups milk
2 cups stock, vegetable water, or bouillon made with cubes	¼ cup skim-milk solids
4 medium potatoes, finely diced	2 Tbs. chopped watercress, parsley, or chives for garnish
dash of pepper	
½ tsp. salt	

Dice salt pork as fine as possible and render slowly in heavy soup kettle over low heat until crisp and golden brown. Remove pork bits with slotted spoon, drain them on a paper towel, and reserve. Raise heat under pork drippings to moderate and cook chopped onion until tender and light brown—4 or 5 minutes. Add stock, diced potatoes, salt, and pepper. With kettle covered, bring to a boil; then lower heat and simmer until potatoes are tender—7 or 8 minutes. Stir in drained salmon or tuna fish, milk, and milk solids. Stir over moderate heat until bubbles form around sides of pan; then remove immediately from source of heat. Do not let it boil. Pour into heated bowls and sprinkle with salt pork bits and green garnish. *Serves 6 to 8.*

Preparing Clams for Chowders

If clams in their shells come your way, put them in the bottom of a large kettle or dishpan, cover them with water, and add a handful—about ⅓ cup—of cornmeal. Leave them overnight, if possible, or for at least 3 to 4 hours. They will clean themselves inside and out, although you should still scrub the shells under running water, scraping two at a time against each other to remove the patina.

Put the cleaned clams in the bottom of a dry kettle or pan and pop them in a 350° oven until they open. With a strong, sharp knife sever the muscles at both sides near the hinges. Do this over a bowl or pan to catch the juices, and use whatever juice may have escaped into the pan while the clams were in the oven. Remove the hard, dark parts of the clam meat but don't throw them away. Chop them for use in the chowder.

Manhattan Clam Chowder

2 cups clam meat	vegetable water
¼ cup chopped salt pork—or 4 slices chopped bacon	½ tsp. pepper pinch each of cayenne, powdered sage, and thyme
½ cup chopped onion	
2 cups diced raw potatoes	salt to taste
1 Tbs. chopped green pepper	(2 Tbs. yeast flakes or brewers' yeast)
2 Tbs. chopped celery	
2 cups stewed tomatoes or tomato juice	

Wash clams in about 2 cups of clean water and save the water, straining it if it appears sandy. Brown salt pork or bacon slowly in heavy soup kettle until crisp. Remove pieces and reserve. Add to the drippings the chopped onion and chopped hard parts of clams, stir, and cook for 2 minutes. Add potatoes, green pepper, and celery and cover with the water in which you washed the clams. If this does not cover sufficiently, add enough vegetable water to do so. Heat to boiling, lower heat, and simmer until potatoes are tender but not soft. Add soft parts of clams, tomatoes (or juice), seasonings, and yeast. Simmer for 3 to 5 minutes. Sprinkle reserved bits of salt pork or bacon over bowlfuls when serving. *Serves 6 to 8.*

New England Clam Chowder

If they are available, the large quahogs make the most flavorsome chowder. These should be chopped or ground after brief cooking.

1 qt. of shucked large clams	2 Tbs. butter
2 cups cold water	2 Tbs. whole-wheat or unbleached flour
¼ lb. chopped salt pork	4 cups scalded milk
½ cup chopped onion	½ cup skim-milk solids
3 cups diced raw potatoes	salt and pepper to taste

Wash clams in water and save water, straining it if it appears sandy. (If you are using quahogs, boil them in the water a few minutes after washing and straining. Save the liquid.) Grind or chop hard parts of clams. Brown the chopped salt pork slowly until brown and crisp. Remove pieces and reserve. Add to drippings the onions and chopped hard parts of clams, stir, and cook for 3 minutes—a little longer if not tender by then. Add potatoes and reserved clam liquid, stir, and simmer until potatoes are tender but not soft. Add the soft parts of clams. In a separate saucepan or double boiler, melt the butter, blend with the flour, and stir in scalded milk and milk solids until mixture begins to thicken slightly. Add and stir this into the chowder and keep it hot until serving. Do not let it boil. Season to taste. Sprinkle bits of crisp salt pork over bowls when serving. *Serves 6 to 8.*

Creamed Soups

If it is creamed, almost any soup can be made more meaningfully nutritious, especially for growing children and the elderly. The protein and calcium of milk are needed by young bodies and by the brittle bones of those in advancing years.

National surveys reveal that high-protein diets are particularly important to the elderly. However, because of ill-fitting dentures and a number of other reasons—economic and social—they may not eat meat in the quantities nutritionists recommend, and they frequently resent drinking milk. Creamed soups (and puddings—see index) are an excellent way of maintaining protective protein-calcium reserves among the senior set.

If overweight is a problem, creamed soups can still provide essential proteins and calcium without excessive calories. Make them with liquefied skim-milk solids instead of whole milk, using at least a third to a half more of the solids than the usual box directions specify.

Basic Rule for Making Cream Soups

3 Tbs. whole-wheat or unbleached flour	2 cups any stock or soup, with or without vegetables
3 Tbs. butter or margarine, melted	salt and pepper if needed
2 cups milk plus 2 Tbs. skim-milk solids	

Add flour slowly to melted butter in top of double boiler, stirring to a smooth paste. Scald milk with skim-milk solids and add slowly, stirring to avoid lumps. Cook but do not boil over boiling water or very low heat until well blended—about 10 minutes. Heat stock or soup and add. Season to taste. The addition of 1 to 2 tablespoons of yeast flakes or brewers' yeast per serving will provide even better nutrition. *Serves 4.*

Individual Cream Soups

Cream of Asparagus Soup

2 bunches green asparagus	2 Tbs. butter or margarine
2 cups (vegetable) water	2 Tbs. whole-wheat or unbleached flour
5 cups any stock, vegetable water, or bouillon made with cubes	½ cup light cream or whole milk—warm
1 Tbs. chopped onion	salt and pepper to taste
1 tsp. chopped parsley	(2–4 Tbs. yeast flakes or brewers' yeast)
½ cup chopped green celery with leaves	

Remove the tender tips of the asparagus and reserve. Cut stalks into 1-inch pieces, or smaller, and boil them in the (vegetable) water for 5 minutes. Add the stalks and liquid to boiling stock along with the onion, parsley, and celery. Simmer for 20 minutes; then put through a food mill or force through a sieve. Return to low heat. In a separate saucepan melt butter, add flour, and mix to a smooth paste. Add warm cream or milk slowly, stirring to prevent lumps. Stir cream sauce into simmering stock. Add reserved uncooked tips, and simmer (do not boil) for 5 minutes, until the tips are tender. Season and stir in yeast. *Serves 6 to 8.*

Cream of Beet Soup

1 cup diced raw beets	2 cups milk
½ cup chopped onions	¼ cup skim-milk solids
½ cup diced raw carrots	salt and pepper to taste
2 cups vegetable water	(1–2 Tbs. yeast flakes or brewers' yeast)
2 eggs, well-beaten	

Cover vegetables with vegetable water and cook until beets are tender—about 15 to 20 minutes. You may rub the vegetables through a sieve, or let them remain in dice. Lower heat. Beat eggs with milk and milk solids and add slowly to soup, stirring over low heat until soup thickens. Season to taste (and add yeast). *Serves 4.*

Cream of Greens Soup

1 lb. greens, individual or mixed—spinach, beet tops, and/or Swiss chard	3 Tbs. unbleached or whole-wheat flour
1 head of lettuce	1¾ cups warm milk
4 cups stock, vegetable water, or bouillon made with cubes	⅓ cup skim-milk solids
3 Tbs. butter or margarine	½ tsp. salt pinch of pepper or paprika

Wash greens; then cook them in their own moisture or in very little water. While they are cooking, chop or shred lettuce and add to greens at the end of 10 minutes. Cook for another 5 minutes. Drain, reserving water; then force the greens through a food mill or sieve. Add stock and reserved water and simmer over low heat while you make cream sauce: Melt butter, blend with flour, slowly add warm milk, milk solids, and seasonings and stir over low heat until thickened. Stir cream sauce into soup pot and correct seasonings if necessary. *Serves 6 to 8.*

Dry-Legume Soups

A variety of hearty, delicious, nutritious soups can be made from the dry beans, lentils, and peas so economically available in markets and so eminently storable on pantry shelves. It's a good idea to keep an assortment on hand for such times as you may have a fowl carcass, a ham bone, or the end of a smoked tongue to add flavor and nutritive value to a satisfying, popular soup.

Soaking dry legumes overnight is a strong habit, but it can and should be broken. This habit is usually accompanied by another one—discarding the water in which the legumes were soaked. When you do this, you discard a high percentage of food value. So if habit is too strong to break and you feel you must soak dry beans and the like overnight, at least restrain yourself from automatically pouring the water down the sink. Let it stay. Add more, if necessary, when you cook the soup. You'll be preserving proteins, vitamins, and minerals along with the carbohydrates.

The cause of tenderness is served when dry legumes are cooked until they are soft.

Another habit which deserves to be broken is the one of adding flour to thicken a legume soup. Nicely thick purées are achieved by putting up to half of the cooked legumes through a food mill. If you want extra body, you can achieve it—and extra nutrition—by adding a few tablespoons of wheat germ or yeast flakes to the soup after it has been puréed and returned to the stove for reheating.

Cooking times for legumes vary according to the softness of your local water and the type of legume you are using: Dry limas take less time to cook than dry navy beans, and split peas or lentils less than whole. (Some packaged brands come precooked.)

Basic Recipe for
Making Soup from Dry Legumes

8 cups boiling vegetable water	½ cup celery with leaves
2 cups dry legumes (split or whole peas, lentils, black, kidney, lima, navy, or other beans)	½ cup chopped or diced carrots
	1 tsp. brown sugar
	salt (if needed)
	pepper to taste
1 bay leaf	
½ cup chopped or sliced onions	
a ham bone, end piece of tongue, fowl carcass, 2-inch cube of salt pork, or 2 slices bacon	

Wash and pick over legumes, drain, and then drop slowly into boiling vegetable water. Try not to interrupt the boil. Add bay leaf, onions, whatever bone or meat you are using. Cover kettle and simmer for 2 to 3 hours, until legumes are tender and their skins crack when you blow on a few taken up in a spoon. Remove bay leaf and bone or meat. If you have time, allow soup to cool until any fat can be skimmed off top. Add celery, carrots, brown sugar. Simmer for 20 minutes. With small sieve or slotted spoon remove and reserve about half of the legumes. Put the rest through a food mill or force through a sieve. Combine purée with the unmashed legumes, bring soup to serving heat, and season to taste. If there are any bits of lean ham, tongue, or fowl clinging to the bones you removed, shred these and add them to the soup. *Serves 4 to 6.*

Serving Hints

Pea or lentil soup: Garnish with wheat germ or whole-wheat croutons.
Black bean soup: Add 1 Tbs. sherry per adult serving, along with slices of hard-cooked eggs and thin lemon wheels.
Navy bean soup: Add cubes of ham or tongue.
Kidney bean soup: Stir in ½ tsp. chili powder 20 minutes before serving.

Any legume soup becomes a hearty one-course luncheon when you add slices or chunks of frankfurters or knockwurst. For even better nutrition, add cubes of broiled liver—or liver dumplings (page 53). Smoked brewers' yeast—½ to 1 teaspoon per portion—lends extra tang and much nutritional value to most of the hearty soups, particularly those made from legumes.

A Word about Soybeans

Much nonsense has been written about soy, as a source of protein which, the public is now convinced, can replace eggs, meat, fish, fowl, and other high quality animal proteins. Soy is—for a vegetable protein—unusually efficient, but not as efficient as meat, milk, fowl and fish proteins. It lacks Vitamin B12, which is a serious deficit not encountered with animal proteins; and it is low in certain important minerals. Its chief values are: it is better quality protein than any other from a vegetable source; and it works nicely with (complements) the better proteins of animal origin. This is to say that soy makes a fine extender for hamburger or meat loaf, where its inadequacies are covered by the more efficient protein of an animal source; but it should not be used as a substitute for meat. Its amino acid balances are *not* satisfactory though they are the mainstay of poor countries where meat and milk products are scarce.

Dry soybeans are exempt from the no-soaking rule, as some form of pretreatment is desirable to neutralize their somewhat unfamiliar flavor and to shorten the cooking time. They can be soaked overnight—3 cups of water to each cup of soybeans. Or they can be covered with water, frozen solid, and kept in the freezer until used. Freezing does not detract from their nutritive value, but reduces cooking time and offers a handy way to have soybeans available on short notice.

Purée of Dry Soybeans

2 cups dry soybeans soaked overnight in 6 cups water, or frozen in 2 cups water	⅛ tsp. black pepper
	½ clove garlic, minced or pressed
(4 cups vegetable water, if soybeans were frozen)	1 cup milk
	¼ cup skim-milk solids
¼ cup chopped celery with leaves	1 Tbs. whole-wheat flour
2–4 Tbs. chopped onion	1 cup rich stock or bouillon made with 2 beef cubes
1 tsp. salt	2 slices bacon—or 2 Tbs. butter

If you have soaked the soybeans, bring them to just below a boil in the soaking water, and simmer, covered, for 3 to 4 hours. If you have frozen them, drop the frozen block into 4 cups of boiling vegetable water. When boiling point is reached, lower heat and simmer for 2 hours.

At the end of the cooking period, add chopped celery, onion, salt, pepper, and garlic and simmer for 30 minutes. Force through food mill or sieve and return to pot. Combine milk, milk solids, and flour and stir into simmering purée. Add and stir stock. In separate skillet, fry bacon until crisp, drain, and reserve both bacon and drippings. Taste the soup. If you find it too dry, add some of the bacon drippings or stir in 2 tablespoons of butter. Taste again and correct seasonings if necessary. Serve in bowls or plates and crumble the crisp bacon over them as garnish. *Serves 4 to 6.*

(For even better nutrition, add up to 1 tablespoon of yeast flakes per serving and/or sprinkle with wheat germ.)

Cold Soups

On a hot summer day appetites may lag but nutritional requirements remain constant. A refreshing, cooling soup replenishes minerals which may be lost via the pores and also provides proteins and vitamins to compensate for spent energies.

Tomato-Cottage Cheese Soup

1 can (10 ounces) condensed tomato soup or purée	¼ tsp. black pepper
	dash of cayenne
2 cups milk	½ cup fine-curd cottage cheese
½ cup skim-milk solids	2 Tbs. chopped onion
1 Tbs. lemon juice	1 Tbs. chopped chives
½ tsp. salt	1 tsp. chopped parsley

Put condensed soup in mixing bowl and stir until smooth. Combine milk with milk solids and add. Stir until well blended. Add lemon juice and seasonings. Stir or beat until thoroughly mixed. Combine cottage cheese, onion, chives, and parsley and spoon into soup like dumplings. Chill in refrigerator for ½ hour or more. If desired, garnish with thin slices of unpeeled cucumbers or radishes. *Serves 4.*

Cucumber Soup

2 cucumbers	2 cups stock, bouillon made with chicken cubes, or 1 can consommé diluted with ⅔ cup water
1 onion	
1 cup (vegetable) water	
1 tsp. salt	1 cup sour cream
⅛ tsp. pepper	1 Tbs. chopped chives or parsley
½ bay leaf—or 1 Tbs. chopped fresh dill	
3 Tbs. whole-wheat or unbleached flour	(1 Tbs. grated lemon rind)

Slice unpeeled cucumbers in half lengthwise and scoop out seeds. Dice cucumbers and onion, cover with water, add salt, pepper, and bay leaf (or dill), and bring to the boiling point. (Remove bay leaf.) Make a smooth paste of the flour and about ½ cup of the stock, and stir into remainder of stock. Stir until well blended, and add to boiling cucumber and onion mixture. Simmer for 10 minutes. Cool slightly; then force through sieve or food mill and let cool to room temperature. Add sour cream, stir well, and chill in the refrigerator. Serve in chilled bowls and garnish with chopped chives or parsley (and grated lemon rind). *Serves 4.*

6
The Wonderful One-dish Meal

Modern home cooks take kindly to the one-dish meal for entertaining and for family approval. Nutritionists take kindly to it, too, especially if it is served with a green salad and a simple dessert.

Many casseroles, stews, and skillet recipes can be prepared in advance, requiring only last-minute heating, and this one fact alone is enough to endear them to busy housewives. Equally busy children also welcome the one-dish meal, for it permits them to leave the table quickly so they can get on with their jobs as television critics and gunslingers.

Aside from its advantages in time and convenience, the one-dish meal provides an attractive vehicle for nutritional treasures otherwise scorned or merely tolerated. The violent vegetable hater somehow relaxes his prejudice when greens, yellows, or other edible colors are absorbed into the melting pot of a handsome casserole or aromatic stew. The milk refuser (this may be an older child—say, one around 60) sees no harm in a creamy, bubbling dish brought to the table from the oven. The meat rejecter (again, perhaps an oldster) doesn't mind meat nearly so much when nothing has to be cut with a knife or chewed with blunt, painful, or imitation teeth.

Casserole and Skillet Dishes

Liver With Brown Rice

1 medium onion, chopped
3 Tbs. butter or margarine
1 lb. beef, calf, or chicken liver cut into small pieces
3 Tbs. wheat germ
1½ cups stock (pages 30–31)
2 Tbs. whole-wheat flour
2½ cups cooked brown rice
1 Tbs. chopped parsley
½ tsp. salt
⅛ tsp. pepper
pinch of oregano or basil

Sauté onion in 1 tablespoon of the melted butter until well coated and glazed but not brown. Melt 2 tablespoons butter in same skillet. Dredge liver in wheat germ and fry, turning once, for 2 to 5 minutes (the longer time for beef liver). Combine stock with flour; add liver and all other ingredients. Mix well. Put into lightly greased casserole and bake at 350° for 20 minutes, or until piping hot. *Serves 4 to 6.*

Fish Pie

3 Tbs. butter or margarine
3 Tbs. unbleached flour
2 cups warm milk
½ cup skim-milk solids
1 tsp. salt
⅛ tsp. pepper
½ lb. grated unprocessed yellow cheese
2 Tbs. chopped onions
1 large red or green pepper, chopped
1½ lb. any fish fillet cut into bite-size pieces
½ cup wheat germ

In saucepan, melt butter, add flour, and blend until smooth. Stir in warm milk, milk solids, salt, and pepper, and heat, stirring, until mixture is thick and smooth. Add all but ¼ cup of the grated cheese and stir until melted. Add chopped onions and peppers, lower heat, and continue to cook without boiling while you lightly grease a casserole. Sprinkle bottom of casserole with half of the wheat germ; then alternate layers of fish and sauce. Sprinkle top with remaining wheat germ and grated cheese. Bake at 350°, uncovered, until cheese melts and browns. *Serves 4 to 6.*

Casserole Corned Beef and Cabbage

1 small head green cabbage, shredded
1 cup lightly salted water
2 Tbs. butter or margarine
2 Tbs. unbleached flour
1½ cups milk
⅓ cup skim-milk solids
1 lb. lean cooked corned beef, cut into pieces (or 1-pound can corned beef)
½ cup grated unprocessed yellow cheese
¼ cup wheat germ

Cook shredded cabbage in salted water until barely tender—about 5 minutes. Drain and reserve cabbage. Melt butter, blend with flour, and add milk and milk solids. Stir until sauce thickens. Lightly grease casserole and arrange layers of cabbage, corned beef, and most of the cheese. Pour cream sauce over this and sprinkle with wheat germ and remaining cheese. Bake at 350° for 30 minutes, until cheese melts and browns. *Serves 4.*

Pork and Rice

1 lb. lean pork
2 cups chopped onions
1 cup chopped celery
1 cup chopped green pepper
2 Tbs. cooking oil
4 cups stewed tomatoes
1 tsp. brown sugar
1 tsp. salt
¼ tsp. pepper
1 cup uncooked brown rice
1 cup grated unprocessed yellow cheese

Trim pork closely and cut into small cubes. Heat fat trimmings in large skillet until bottom is coated enough to brown the meat on all sides. Remove and reserve meat, discarding the fat. In the same skillet, sauté onions, celery, and green pepper in hot cooking oil for 3 or 4 minutes. Drain vegetables and combine with tomatoes, sugar, and seasonings. Add uncooked rice and mix well. Cover bottom of casserole with half of the vegetable-rice mixture; add half of the browned pork and half of the grated cheese. Repeat these layers, topping them with the remaining cheese. Cover tightly and bake at 350° for 1½ hours. Uncover and bake 30 minutes more. *Serves 4 to 6.*

Fredericks's Casserole

2 large sweet
potatoes, or 4
small ones
3 Tbs. milk
1 Tbs. skim-milk
solids
2 Tbs. wheat germ

1 Tbs. butter
salt and pepper
1 Tbs. orange juice
2 cups ground or
minced cooked ham
8 slices bacon
4 eggs

Boil sweet potatoes in their jackets until soft; then peel and mash the pulp with milk, milk solids, wheat germ, butter, and seasonings to taste. Mix with orange juice. Lightly grease a casserole and line it with half of the mashed potato mixture. Spread all but 4 tablespoons of the ham over the sweet potato lining. Shape 4 cones of the remaining sweet potatoes, denting the peaks with a spoon. Put a tablespoonful of ham in each crater. Put in 325° oven while you fry bacon until it is crisp and poach the eggs. Place a poached egg on top of each potato crater and garnish with bacon. *Serves 4.*

Stuffed Cabbage Leaves

1 cup uncooked
brown rice
4 cups boiling lightly
salted water
1 cup diced lean pork
1 cup diced lean beef
1 medium onion
½ tsp. nutmeg
1 tsp. lemon juice
2 eggs, beaten

(1–2 Tbs. wheat germ,
yeast flakes, or
brewers' yeast)
12 large cabbage
leaves
2 cups stewed or
canned whole
peeled tomatoes
1 cup sour cream

Cook rice in briskly boiling water for 15 minutes. Drain. Put it through the grinder with pork, beef, and onion. Add nutmeg, lemon juice, and beaten eggs (and wheat germ or yeast), and mix thoroughly. Wilt cabbage leaves until they are pliable by pouring a little boiling water over them. Remove tough core at base of leaves. Put 2 tablespoons of the meat mixture in center of each leaf and fold over the edges, starting to roll at the thick end of the leaves. Fasten securely with toothpicks. Put cabbage rolls in lightly greased baking dish or casserole and cover with tomatoes. Bake, covered, at 300° for 1 hour. Remove from oven, drain off liquid, and combine it with the sour cream for a sauce. *Serves 6.*

Note: A somewhat more nutritious but equally good-tasting recipe would be to omit the pork and substitute 1 cup of ground beef

liver, kidney, or heart. Tomato sauce, soup, or purée may be used in place of the sour cream.

Good-Nutrition Macaroni and Cheese

2 cups (½ lb.) enriched
elbow macaroni*
2 qts. boiling water
with 2 tsp. salt
2 Tbs. butter or
margarine
2 Tbs. unbleached or
whole-wheat flour
2 cups warm milk
¼ cup skim-milk
solids
salt, pepper, or
paprika to taste

2 eggs
¼ lb. chipped
beef—or 1 to 2 cups
any leftover cooked
meat, fish, or fowl
1 cup grated
unprocessed yellow
cheese
½ cup wheat germ
½ cup coarse
whole-wheat bread
crumbs

Drop macaroni slowly into boiling salted water and cook until tender but not soft—about 7 to 10 minutes. Drain. Melt butter in saucepan, mix into smooth paste with flour, and slowly add warm milk and milk solids. Season to taste and stir over low heat until mixture is smooth and begins to thicken. Remove from heat and cool slightly. Stir eggs with fork and beat them into the sauce. In lightly greased casserole arrange layers of cooked macaroni, sauce, meat, wheat germ, and cheese. Top with sprinkling of cheese and whole-wheat crumbs. Bake at 375° until cheese melts and begins to brown. *Serves 4 to 6.*

Baked Stuffed Peppers

4 large bell peppers
1 lb. chopped
beef—or 1 lb. mixed
chopped beef and
country sausage
1 cup cooked brown
rice
¼ cup wheat germ
¼ cup grated
unprocessed yellow
cheese

1 egg
½ clove garlic, minced
or pressed
1 cup Italian meat
sauce—your own
(page 43) or
canned

Cut (and save) stem ends from peppers and remove seeds. Brown chopped beef or meat mixture slowly in its own fat, pouring off excess and crumbling it with a fork as it cooks. Mix cooked meat with all other ingredients except spaghetti sauce. Stuff peppers with the

*See note, page 23

mixture. Stand peppers upright in lightly greased baking dish, surround them with ½ cup of water, cap with stem ends, and bake at 350° until peppers are tender. Serve with spaghetti sauce. *Serves 4.*

Seafood Polenta

6 cups lightly salted vegetable water
1 cup undegerminated yellow cornmeal
¼ cup wheat germ
6 slices bacon
2 medium onions, chopped
¼ cup chopped green pepper

1 cup Italian meat sauce—your own (page 43) or canned
1 lb. cooked shrimp, lobster, or crab meat—or 1 lb. cooked fillets—or 2 cans tuna fish or salmon

Bring vegetable water to a boil and slowly add cornmeal and wheat germ. Cook over low heat, stirring, until mushy. Brown bacon until almost crisp and remove from pan. Fry onions and pepper in bacon drippings for 2 minutes, remove with slotted spoon, and combine with spaghetti sauce and seafood. Line a lightly greased casserole with about two-thirds of the cornmeal, fill with seafood mixture, and top with remaining cornmeal. Arrange bacon on top and bake at 350° for 15 to 20 minutes, until bacon is crisp. *Serves 4 to 6.*

Enriched Tamale Pie

1½ cups undegerminated yellow cornmeal
½ cup wheat germ
1 qt. salted vegetable water
1 Tbs. olive oil
2 Tbs. minced onions
½ clove garlic, minced or pressed
1 lb. chopped beef

2 cups stewed tomatoes
1 cup stock or bouillon
½ to 1 tsp. chili powder
pinch of basil
2 eggs, lightly beaten
1 cup pitted black olives

Stir cornmeal and wheat germ slowly into boiling vegetable water and cook over low heat, stirring, until mushy. Set aside to cool. Sauté onions and garlic in olive oil for 2 minutes. Add chopped beef and break with a fork as it browns. Mix meat with stewed tomatoes and stock, and season with chili powder and basil. Stir lightly beaten eggs into cooled

cornmeal mush and combine with meat mixture and olives. Pour into lightly greased casserole and bake at 350° until piping hot—or keep hot in a chafing dish. If you prefer, you can press half of the cornmeal-egg mixture into the bottom of the casserole, fill with the meat mixture, and top with remaining cornmeal formed into walnut-size balls. *Serves 4 to 6.*

Seafood (or Variety) Rarebit

Welsh rarebit is a fine milk and cheese dish. The addition of eggs and your choice of seafood or organ meat makes it an exceptionally high protein recipe.

½ lb. coarsely grated yellow cheese
2 Tbs. butter or margarine, melted
¾ cup milk
¼ cup skim-milk solids
2 eggs, lightly beaten
¼ tsp. salt

pinch cayenne
1 cup or more oysters, clams, cooked boneless fish; or cooked diced liver, kidney, brains, heart
4 slices whole-wheat bread, toasted

Add cheese to melted butter over low heat. As cheese melts, gradually add milk, milk solids, lightly beaten eggs, and seasonings, stirring constantly. When smooth and hot (don't let it boil) add the seafood or diced organ meat. Serve on toasted whole-wheat bread. *Serves 4.*

Oyster (or Clam) and Eggplant Casserole

Eggplant is not an especially exciting vegetable nutritionally, but it is delicious, low-calorie, and nice and bulky—very fine for extending recipes. Used in combination with the high proteins, vitamins, and minerals of oysters or clams and cheese, with the vitamin C of tomatoes, and the altogether virtuous qualities of wheat germ instead of the usual bread crumbs, eggplant becomes the proud bearer of superb nutrition.

1 medium eggplant, peeled and cut in ¼-inch slices
3 large tomatoes, peeled and thinly sliced—or 2 cups canned tomatoes
2 cups grated yellow cheese

1 cup or more raw oysters or clams, coarsely chopped
½ cup wheat germ
2 Tbs. butter or margarine, melted

Alternate layers of eggplant, tomatoes, grated cheese, and chopped oysters or clams in a lightly greased casserole. Sprinkle with wheat germ and melted butter or margarine. Bake at 375° for 1 hour. *Serves 4 to 6.*

Note: This recipe can also be used with 1 cup or more diced cooked lamb instead of oysters or clams.

Veal-Eggplant Parmigiana

Good nutrition suggests that you combine two popular items usually served separately in Italian restaurants. Note also that this recipe calls for a meat sauce instead of the usual tomato sauce.

2 eggs	(about) 3 Tbs. olive oil
2 Tbs. milk or cream	2½–3 cups Italian
1 lb. Italian style veal cutlets—very thin, very lean	meat sauce (recipe follows)
1 medium eggplant, peeled and cut into ½-inch slices	½ lb. Mozzarella cheese grated Parmesan cheese
½ cup wheat germ	
1 clove garlic, minced	

Beat eggs with milk or cream. Dip veal in beaten egg, then in wheat germ. Do the same with the sliced eggplant. Brown minced garlic in 2 tablespoons olive oil. Remove garlic. Brown prepared veal for 5 to 6 minutes on each side and remove. Add remaining oil and brown prepared eggplant for 3 to 4 minutes on each side. Cover bottom of baking dish with 1 cup of sauce. Alternate veal and eggplant in layers, cover with 1 cup of sauce, and top with thin slices of Mozzarella. Pour remaining sauce over this and sprinkle with Parmesan cheese. Bake at 300° until Mozzarella melts and bubbles. *Serves 4 to 6.*

Italian Meat Sauce

1 clove garlic, minced or pressed	2 cups (1 large can) Italian tomato purée
1 small onion, chopped	1 small can Italian tomato paste
1 small green pepper, chopped	pinch of basil
2 Tbs. olive oil	salt and pepper to taste
½ lb. ground beef (up to half of this may be ground pork)	(¼–½ cup dry red wine)

Sauté garlic, onion, and pepper in olive oil for 3 minutes. Add and brown ground meat, crumbling with a fork as it cooks. Pour off excess oil and drippings. Add purée, paste, and seasonings. Cover pan, lower heat, and simmer very slowly for at least 1 hour. If you have time for this to simmer longer (the secret of really good Italian sauce), you may add, if or when it seems necessary, up to a cup of tomato purée, juice, or stewed tomatoes. Just before sauce is to be served, stir in wine and simmer for 5 minutes.

Fish Bake

4 large pieces (about 2 lbs.) any fish fillet—flounder, perch, sole, swordfish	1 cup cottage cheese
	½ cup sour cream
	¾ tsp. salt
	⅛ tsp. pepper
	⅔ cup milk
1½ cups mashed potatoes	1 Tbs. butter
	⅓ cup wheat germ

Place two slices of fish in a lightly greased casserole. Mix together the mashed potatoes, cottage cheese, sour cream, and seasonings. Spread half of this mixture over fish and repeat the layers. Pour milk over the layers, dot with butter, and sprinkle with wheat germ. Bake at 350° for 30 minutes. *Serves 4.*

Casserole Espagnole

1 lb. lean beef— chuck, shin, round	½ cup chopped onions
	3 Tbs. cooking oil
1 tsp. unseasoned granulated meat tenderizer	½ tsp. salt
	⅛ tsp. pepper
	1½ cups cooked brown rice
1 large green pepper, coarsely chopped	1½ cups stewed tomatoes
1 cup chopped green celery	½ cup grated yellow cheese

Tenderize beef for 1 hour. Sauté chopped vegetables in 2 tablespoons of the cooking oil until wilted. Remove vegetables from skillet with slotted spoon. Add remaining tablespoon of oil to skillet. Cut tenderized beef into small cubes, season with salt and pepper, and brown quickly in the hot oil, turning frequently. Mix sautéed vegetables and beef with cooked rice and put into lightly greased baking dish. Pour tomatoes over this mixture, sprinkle with grated cheese, and bake for 40 minutes at 350°. *Serves 4 to 6.*

High-Protein-Vitamin Bake

1 lb. pork sausage meat
4 cups milk
½ cup skim-milk solids
½ cup undegerminated yellow cornmeal
½ cup wheat germ
2 Tbs. yeast flakes
1 tsp. salt
1 cup grated yellow cheese
4 eggs, separated

Shape sausage meat into flat patties and brown slowly without adding fat—5 to 6 minutes per side. Remove and drain on paper towel. Combine milk with milk solids and scald 3 cups of the mixture. Slowly stir in cornmeal, wheat germ, yeast flakes, salt, and grated cheese. Mix well and cook over low heat, stirring continuously, until cheese melts and mixture thickens—about 5 minutes. Remove from heat and stir in remaining cup of (cold) milk. Allow this to cool further. Beat egg yolks until light and frothy and add them to the cereal mixture, blending thoroughly. Beat egg whites until stiff and fold into mixture. Pour into lightly greased casserole, arrange partially cooked patties on top, and bake at 350° for 40 minutes. *Serves 4 to 6.*

Chili con Carne

2 cups (1 lb.) dried kidney beans
1½ qts. boiling (vegetable) water
1 tsp. salt
1 bay leaf
½ cup chopped onions
1 clove garlic, minced
2 Tbs. cooking oil
1 lb. chopped beef
1½ cups stewed tomatoes
2 Tbs. yeast flakes
1 tsp. salt
1 tsp. brown sugar
2–6 tsp. chili powder, depending on how spicy you like chili to be
½ small head lettuce, shredded
1 large onion, finely chopped
1 cup pitted ripe olives

Drop washed kidney beans slowly into boiling water, trying not to disturb the boil. Stir in salt and add bay leaf. Reduce heat to slow boil and cook until skin of bean cracks when blown on—about 1½ to 2 hours. Drain, reserving bean water. In large, heavy kettle, sauté onions and garlic in oil for 2 or 3 minutes. Add chopped beef and brown, breaking beef with a fork as it cooks. Add tomatoes and 1 cup of the bean water, and stir in yeast flakes, salt, brown sugar, and chili powder. Cook for 20 minutes. Add kidney beans and stir to mix well. If mixture seems too thick, add more bean water (or unseasoned stock). Simmer 30 minutes longer. This can be served immediately, or made ahead for reheating. The flavor intensifies on standing. If you reheat, add a little more yeast flakes to compensate for vitamin loss. Serve in bowls and garnish with shredded lettuce, chopped onions, and olives. *Serves 6 to 8.*

Pilaf

¾ cup uncooked brown rice
3 Tbs. cooking oil
2 Tbs. chopped onion
¼ cup chopped green pepper
2½ cups stewed tomatoes
1 tsp. salt
⅛ tsp. paprika
½ tsp. brown sugar
pinch cayenne
1 cup or more cooked shrimp, diced cooked fish, fowl, or meat of any kind
½ cup wheat germ
½ cup grated yellow cheese
2 hard-cooked eggs

Toast rice in skillet in 1 tablespoon of the oil, shaking or stirring to coat the grains. In another skillet sauté onions and green pepper in remaining oil for 2 minutes. Combine with toasted rice, add tomatoes and seasonings, and simmer for 20 minutes, stirring occasionally. Remove from heat and set aside for 30 minutes so rice can absorb moisture. Mix with cooked fish or meat; bake (350°) in lightly greased casserole for 30 minutes, until rice is tender. Sprinkle with wheat germ and grated cheese and return to oven until cheese melts and starts to brown. Garnish with sliced hard-cooked egg. *Serves 4 to 6.*

Curried Shrimp

3–4 qts. water
1 tsp. salt
½ tsp. black pepper
¼ tsp. cayenne
1 clove garlic, minced or pressed
4 or 5 stalks celery with leaves
1 onion, sliced
2 lbs. shrimp
1 Tbs. lemon juice

Boil water and seasonings together for 15 minutes. Add shrimp and lemon juice, and boil for 5 minutes. Remove from heat and let shrimp cool in cooking water. Shell and devein.

½ cup finely chopped onions
⅛ lb. butter
4 Tbs. unbleached flour
1½–3 tsp. curry powder
1 tsp. salt
½ tsp. brown sugar
⅛ tsp. cinnamon
¼ tsp. powdered ginger
2 cups hot, lightly seasoned chicken stock—or bouillon, omitting salt from recipe

½ cup chopped firm apple
½ cup seedless raisins
1 cup light cream
2 Tbs. skim-milk solids
2 cups cooked brown rice

Cook onions in butter until glazed. Using wooden spoon to stir, add and blend thoroughly the flour and all seasonings. Add hot stock slowly, stirring until smooth. Add apples, drained raisins, and cooked shrimp. Just before serving, add cream mixed with milk solids and keep the mixture hot without letting it boil. *Serves 4 to 6.*

For a company dinner, pass small bowlfuls of chutney, grated egg white, grated egg yolk, chopped peanuts or cashews, grated onion, shredded coconut, sweet-and-sour sauce.

This recipe can also be used with diced cooked chicken, turkey, veal, or lamb instead of shrimp.

Sukiyaki

Oriental short-cooking of vegetables retains their vitamins, color, and crispness. Made at the table on a Japanese hibachi or in an American electric skillet, this dish is fun for the family as well as excellent nutrition.

4 Tbs. cooking oil
4 cups green celery, cut in ¼-inch diagonal slices
2 thinly sliced onions
1 cup young scallions, cut in 2-inch slices
1 cup coarsely cut green pepper
3 cups thinly sliced mushrooms
1 can drained bamboo shoots

2 tomatoes, thinly sliced
1½ cups stock, concentrated canned consommé, or bouillon made with 2 beef cubes
½ cup soy sauce
4 tsp. brown sugar
1 qt. spinach leaves torn to bite-size pieces
1½ lbs. beefsteak sliced ⅛ inch thick

Heat oil over moderate heat. Add all vegetables except spinach (tomatoes on top), and cook for only 3 or 4 minutes, stirring occasionally. Pour consommé and soy sauce over vegetables and stir. Sprinkle with sugar and stir. Add spinach and wafer-thin slices of beef. Simmer for 5 minutes and serve. *Serves 4 to 6.*

Stews

Stews can be among the easiest, least expensive, and most nutritionally satisfying and popular one-dish meals. Men—even presidents of the United States—dote on them and occasionally take pride in making them. The recipe given here is basic and sound. Although it specifies beef, any meat the family likes—and some they think they don't like—can be used. Beef heart, for example, makes a delicious stew. Before daring to offer up a whole-hearted stew if your family is unaccustomed to this excellent food, try mixing it with beef at first. Tenderize cubes of heart by marinating them for 1 hour or more in a liquid tenderizer or by sprinkling with a granulated tenderizer.

Fredericks' Basic Beef Stew

2 lbs. lean stew beef (chuck, round) cut into 1½-inch cubes seasoned (salt and pepper) unbleached or whole-wheat flour for dredging
½ cup chopped onions
2 Tbs. cooking oil or rendered beef fat
2 cups boiling vegetable water or unseasoned stock
1 cup stewed tomatoes

2 cups diced potatoes
1 cup each coarsely cut carrots and green beans
½ cup thinly sliced green celery
1 green pepper, coarsely cut
1 Tbs. butter
2–3 Tbs. yeast flakes or brewers' yeast
salt and pepper to taste
(2–4 Tbs. dry red wine)

Dredge beef in seasoned flour and set aside. In large, heavy kettle sauté onions in hot oil or fat until glazed, not brown. Add beef and brown quickly on all sides.* Cover with boiling vegetable water or stock and add stewed tomatoes. Lower heat and simmer, covered, until beef is fork-tender—1 hour or more, depending on cut of beef. In separate saucepans and *very*

*For low-fat diets, let meat cool completely before adding stock and remove all congealed fat with which it may be coated.

little water parboil potatoes, carrots, and beans until tender but not soft. Add these vegetables, along with some of the water in which they were cooked, to the stew pot. Sauté celery and green pepper in butter for 3 minutes and add to stew. Stir in yeast; season to taste. Keep heat low and simmer for 20 minutes more. For adults, add dry red wine for the last 5 minutes of cooking. *Serves 4 to 6.*

Note: Vary the seasonings occasionally with your preferences in herbs. There is no limitation on the varieties of vegetable which may be used. Just remember to cook them very briefly toward the end of the beef simmering time—in a minimum of water—and add some of the water to the stew, saving the rest for future recipes.

Special Chicken Stew

Don't waste a tender chicken on this, unless your family is so fond of what it calls "fricassee" that it pays to take the extra preparation time beyond roasting, broiling, or frying—all good ways of serving young fowl. When the markets offer "stewing" or "soup" chickens at low cost, however, this is your recipe for good nutrition.

1 stewing chicken, 4–6 lbs.	12 or more baby carrots
3 cups vegetable water	12 or more small white onions
2 tsp. salt	1 cup fresh or frozen peas
¼ tsp. black pepper	
3 Tbs. chicken fat or stock skimmings	2 egg yolks, beaten with 2 Tbs. milk and 1 Tbs. skim-milk solids
3 Tbs. unbleached flour	
1 Tbs. brewers' yeast or yeast flakes	

Disjoint chicken and put the pieces slowly into boiling vegetable water seasoned with salt and pepper. Cover pot tightly, lower heat, and simmer until chicken legs are tender—around 2 hours. Let chicken cool in the cooking water. When cool enough to handle, remove chicken, discard the skin, and cut the meat from the bones in fairly large pieces. Reserve the meat and let cooking water chill in refrigerator until fat rises to top. Skim off this surface fat, add to it enough chicken fat to yield 3 tablespoons, and melt it. Blend with flour and yeast and add to cold stock. Stir until smooth. Return to heat and simmer slowly while you cook carrots, onions, and peas in very little water until tender. To simmering stock slowly add beaten egg-milk mixture. Stir until thickened, and add boned chicken and vegetables. Serve with wheat-germ biscuits (page 60). *Serves 4 to 6.*

Beef Stroganoff

This sounds so fancy but is actually so simple that it is a joy to serve to family or guests even on very short notice. If budget doesn't matter, use sirloin or any other choice, tender beef. If budget does matter, use any of the lean cuts—top or bottom round, chuck—and tenderize for 1 hour or more before proceeding.

1½ lbs. lean beef	¼ tsp. basil
2 Tbs. finely chopped or grated onion	sprinkling of nutmeg
	1 Tbs. yeast flakes or brewers' yeast
3 Tbs. butter	1 cup warm sour cream
1 lb. mushrooms, sliced—or 2 cans button mushrooms	2 cups cooked brown or converted rice
½ tsp. salt	
sprinkling of black pepper	

Pound beef until it is very thin and cut into 2-inch squares or 1½- by 4-inch strips. Set aside. Sauté onion in 1 tablespoon of the butter until glazed, not brown. Add beef and sauté until tender—about 5 minutes—turning once or twice until nicely brown. Remove beef to heated plate. Sauté mushrooms in remaining 2 tablespoons of butter—2 or 3 minutes only. Return beef to pan; add and stir seasonings and yeast. Reduce heat. Just before serving, add warm sour cream and stir. Do not let this boil. Serve over rice. This is excellent with Harvard beets or glazed carrots. *Serves 4 to 6.*

7
The Best
Chapter in the Book

During the course of my nutrition broadcasts, I have learned that the instant I mention organ or glandular meats as staples of diet, that is the instant I lose attention—except on the part of the truly nutrition-minded.

The average American's aversion to a long list of foods providing the most superb protective nutrition available is as deeply ingrained as it is incomprehensible. Aside from occasional condescension to calf's liver, chicken liver, cocktail pâté (goose liver), and sweetbreads, the ordinary man, woman, and child in this country goes through life with only a nodding acquaintance with the excellent, protein-rich glandular meats.

What do you suppose the vitamin manufacturers use as source material for many of the pills, tablets, and capsules which have become almost necessities for supplementing American diets? They use livers, kidneys, hearts, and brains of fish and meat animals.

It's hard to trace modern American apathy toward organ meats. Certainly our ancestors had no such apathy, nor do many of the world's current populations—both civilized and primitive. In many parts of the world an animal's vital organs are preferred over the flesh and muscles which constitute American preference. In those parts of the world, especially if the population has not been exposed to our overprocessed, overrefined foods, the general health of the community is far better than ours.

More than one adventurer fallen into Arctic wastes or jungle tangles has been brought back to vigorous life by natives who fed him the heart, liver, or kidneys of a fresh-killed animal. Among hunting tribes in Africa and South America, the glands and organs are presented as choice prizes to the chiefs, the bravest warriors, and the pregnant women.

Properly prepared organ meats are tasty, and there are excellent reasons why they should appear more often on your dinner table. Nature is provident and protective. In her estimation, a living being's heart, pancreas, liver, kidneys, and brains are far more important than its tendons or contour. Consequently, the organs—not the muscles or flesh—are the prime depots and repositories for the best nutrients extracted from food. The organs give the best of nutrients because they get the best of nutrients—topnotch, body-repairing proteins, essential aminos, natural vitamins and minerals. They are minimal in fat and almost devoid of carbohydrates. They contain agents vitally important in the metabolism of fats, the conversion of sugars, the release of essential oxygen, the building of rich blood.

If this book serves no purpose other than to induce you to serve more of the organ meats more often, its author will feel his mission almost accomplished. The "almost" is a necessary qualification. The addition of organ meats to your diet will improve it substantially. If you also reduce your intake of refined sugars and flours and accept the recommendations for breakfasts, breadstuffs, and desserts in other chapters, you will truly be on the road to optimum nutrition.

Brains

We might as well plunge right in and tackle first the organ that comes first in the alphabetical list of glandular meats. Steel yourself, if you're one of those who cringe at the thought or mention of brains as food. Be adventurous and courageous and try at least one of the following recipes at least once. If you do, I'm confident you will try them all. Any kind of brains available from your butcher may be used—calf, beef, lamb, or pork.

To Prepare Brains for Recipes

Wash brains quickly in about a quart of very cold water, or under running water. Remove membranes and drain.

For most recipes, brains do not require precooking. However, palates unfamiliar with their soft texture may prefer them slightly toughened by steaming or simmering. Whenever you precook them by either method, be sure to save (refrigerated) the water in which they cooked. It is teeming with B vitamins and can be added unobtrusively to soups, stews, and stocks.

To steam brains: Put them in a heavy saucepan with ¼ cup of water and 1 tablespoon of vinegar. Cover pan with a tight-fitting lid and steam for 15 minutes.

To simmer brains: Barely cover them with lightly salted water to which you have added 1 tablespoon of vinegar. Simmer gently for 20 minutes. They should never be permitted to boil violently. Their proteins should harden slowly, like the proteins of eggs.

Brain "Oysters"

1 lb. brains	½ tsp. salt
2 eggs, slightly beaten	dash of pepper
	½ cup wheat germ
1 Tbs. milk	oil for deep frying

Prepare brains by method given above. Cut drained brains into pieces about the size of small oysters. Stir beaten eggs with milk, salt, and pepper. Dip "oysters" in this mixture, then in wheat germ. Repeat. Let stand for a few minutes, or refrigerate for ½ hour. Fry in deep, hot oil until golden brown. If you like fried oysters, you'll like these. *Serves 4.*

Brains à la King

1 lb. brains	½ cup chopped green pepper
4 Tbs. butter or margarine	2 Tbs. chopped pimiento or red pepper (sweet)
3 Tbs. unbleached or whole-wheat flour	
2 cups milk	1 Tbs. grated onion
¼ cup skim-milk solids	½ tsp. salt
	⅛ tsp. pepper
½ cup diced green celery	

Steam or simmer brains as described. Drain, and cut or separate into small pieces. Melt 3 tablespoons of butter and blend with flour into a smooth paste. Heat milk and milk solids and add to flour blend, stirring to avoid lumps. Cook over low heat until mixture thickens. Sauté vegetables for 2 minutes in remaining tablespoon of butter and add to white sauce. Season with salt and pepper. Add brains and heat thoroughly without boiling. Serve on whole-wheat toast. If you like chicken à la king, you'll like this. *Serves 4 to 6.*

Note: Timid beginners can add the precooked brains to chicken à la king recipes in any desired proportions.

Western Scrambled Eggs with Brains

2 Tbs. minced green or red pepper	½ lb. brains
	4–6 eggs
1 Tbs. minced onion	¼ cup milk or cream
2 Tbs. bacon drippings or ham fat	1 tsp. soy sauce
	salt and pepper to taste

Sauté pepper and onions in bacon or ham drippings until they are glazed and golden. Dice and add brains and sauté for 10 minutes, stirring to brown evenly. Beat eggs with milk and soy sauce, add to skillet, and scramble. Season to taste. *Serves 4 to 6.*

Brain Canapes

Cold:

1 lb. brains	2–4 Tbs. chili sauce
¼ cup each minced	or catsup
onion, chopped	1 Tbs. mayonnaise
green or red	1 tsp. horse-radish
pepper, chopped	salt, pepper, cayenne
green celery	to taste
3 hard-cooked eggs,	
chopped	

Simmer brains (page 48) and chop or mash with fork. Add and blend in all other ingredients, seasoning to taste. (For variety, add also a dash each of curry powder and powdered ginger.) Serve on whole-wheat crackers or toast rounds. *Makes enough for a fairly large cocktail party.*

Hot:

1 lb. brains	whole wheat bread
2 eggs, slightly	cut into small
beaten	rounds
2 Tbs. wheat germ	deep oil or fat for
½ tsp. salt	frying
⅛ tsp. pepper	sliced pimiento-filled
	olives

Steam or simmer brains (page 48) and grind or chop. Add beaten eggs, wheat germ, and seasonings. Spread on whole-wheat rounds and fry in hot oil or fat until bread is crouton-crisp—about 1 minute. Drain on paper towels and top with slices of stuffed olives. *Makes enough for a fairly large cocktail party.*

Heart

Heart, which is a large muscle as well as an organ, has a texture similar to lean beef, veal, or lamb; but it is far richer than any of these in essential protein, vitamins, and minerals.

Because it is comparatively inexpensive many housewives who are pet lovers are accustomed to buying and preparing heart for their dogs or cats but not for their families. Mama, Papa, and the kids partake of an animal's rump, shoulder, or pelvic area while Fido gnaws happily on its nutrient-filled heart. It may or may not be coincidence that in such families the doctor is usually a more familiar figure around the house than the veterinarian.

Heart is prepared for cooking by washing in cold water and removing the veins and arteries, if the butcher hasn't already removed them.

Sweet and Sour Beef
Heart Stuffed with Brown Rice

1 beef heart (select a	¼ cup cooking oil or
small one, about	melted shortening
2½–3 lbs.)	salt and pepper
1½ cups cooked brown	1 cup water
rice	
2 Tbs. butter or	
margarine, melted	

Wash and trim heart. Combine cooked rice with melted butter and fill heart cavity. Fasten with skewers. In chicken fryer or other deep covered heavy pan, brown heart, turning frequently, in hot cooking oil or shortening. When nicely and evenly browned, add 1 cup of water (be prepared to add more later) and season lightly with salt and pepper. Cover closely and simmer over low to moderate heat until tender—allow 3 to 3½ hours. Peek once in a while and add a little water if necessary. Don't worry about adding water—you'll be using it later for the sauce. When heart is tender, remove it from the pan and keep it warm while you make the sweet and sour sauce:

2 Tbs. butter	4 Tbs. vinegar
2 Tbs. whole-wheat	1 Tbs. honey
flour	1 Tbs. brown sugar
liquid in which heart	1 bay leaf
was cooked plus	2 whole cloves
enough stock or	⅛ tsp. thyme
vegetable water to	salt and pepper
yield 2 cups	

Melt butter and blend with flour until smooth. Gradually add the pan liquid, stirring constantly. Cook over low heat until thickened. Add vinegar, honey, sugar, and seasonings and simmer for 15 minutes. Remove bay leaf and cloves. Return heart to pan and reheat. *Serves 4 to 6.*

Braised Heart with Apples

½ average beef	(about) 1 cup
heart—or 3 pork	unbleached or
hearts, 4 lamb	whole-wheat flour
hearts, or 2 veal	2 Tbs. cooking oil
hearts	4 hard, sweet apples
salt and pepper	¼ cup honey

8 whole cloves	1 small lemon, thinly
2 small bay leaves,	sliced
crushed	½ cup water

Wash and trim heart. Season with salt and pepper, and roll in flour. Brown in hot oil. Quarter and core apples, but do not peel them. Put heart in lightly greased baking dish, surround with apples, and sprinkle with honey, cloves, and crushed bay leaves. Top with slices of lemon, add water, cover tightly, and bake at 300° until heart is tender—beef, 4 hours; others from 2 to 2½ hours. *Serves 4 to 6.*

Kidneys

The people who savor kidneys are usually those with gourmet palates who also appreciate such foods as venison, wild duck, and other bagged fowl—the stronger-tasting, gamy meats. The people who scorn kidneys are usually those who, for example, eat only the breast of chicken or turkey, will try domesticated rabbit (but not any brought home by a hunter) on a dare or to be polite, and, as a rule, don't care too much for lamb.

In order to overcome the prejudice of dainty eaters, kidneys should not taste strong. People with robust tastes will eat them anyway, and presumably the ones who need their nutrients most are the ones who say they'd rather starve—which, in a sense, they do, for their eating preferences are likely to lean toward bland, overstarchy foods.

Kidneys need not taste strong, and they need never be anything but tender. The secret of mildness and tenderness is threefold:

1. Fat-trimming and careful, thorough removal of tubes before putting kidneys into or near water.
2. A little vinegar somewhere in the recipe to neutralize taste—or a marinade of French dressing for about an hour or so before proceeding with a recipe.
3. Short cooking.

To Prepare Kidneys for Cooking

Before washing, split kidneys lengthwise and remove tubes. Trim fat. Wash quickly in cold water and remove membranes. Drain or pat dry.

Beefsteak and Kidney Stew

1 lb. beef kidneys	1½ cups coarsely cut
1 Tbs. vinegar	carrots
1 lb. lean stew beef	1½ cups diced
cut into 1-inch	potatoes
cubes	½–1 cup any other
seasoned unbleached	vegetables,
flour for dredging	individual or
4 Tbs. cooking oil	mixed—beans,
½ cup chopped onions	turnips, celery, etc.
½ cup coarsely cut	salt and pepper
green peppers	
2 cups boiling	
vegetable water or	
stock	

Prepare kidneys as described and cut into ½-inch slices or 1-inch cubes. Sprinkle with vinegar, or marinate in French dressing, and set aside while you make the beef stew: Dredge beef in seasoned flour and brown quickly on all sides in 2 tablespoons of the oil. Add and glaze onions and green peppers. Pour boiling vegetable water or stock over these ingredients, lower heat, and simmer until beef is tender—1 to 1½ hours. Parboil vegetables separately in very little water until not quite tender and add to stew along with some of the cooking waters. Season to taste—a pinch of basil or oregano may be added, if you like these herbs. Now dredge the marinated kidney pieces in seasoned flour, brown quickly in remaining 2 tablespoons of oil, add to stew pot, and simmer for 10 minutes. *Serves 6 to 8.*

Note: This can be converted into a beefsteak and kidney pie by transferring the cooked beef stew to a casserole dish, adding kidneys when they have been browned, topping with biscuit dough (page 61), and baking at 425° until dough is done—about 12 to 15 minutes.

Kidney Diabolo

1 lb. beef kidneys	½ cup boiling water
1 Tbs. vinegar	or unseasoned
½ cup chopped	stock
onions	1 tsp. salt
2 Tbs. cooking oil	¼ tsp. black pepper
½ cup whole-wheat	1½ tsp. dry mustard
or unbleached	½–¾ cup warm sour
flour	cream
2 Tbs. wheat germ	

Prepare kidneys as described and cut into small pieces. Sprinkle with vinegar and let stand for 1 hour in refrigerator. Glaze onions in oil, roll kidneys in mixture of flour and wheat germ, and brown on top of onions for 2 or 3 minutes, turning to brown evenly. Add boiling liquid and seasonings and stir. Simmer for 10 minutes, lower heat, and stir in sour cream. Do not let it boil. *Serves 4.*

Kidney and Meat Loaf

1 lb. beef, veal, pork, or lamb kidneys	½ cup wheat germ
1 Tbs. vinegar	1 egg
½ cup chopped onions	1 tsp. salt
¼ cup chopped green pepper	¼ tsp. black pepper
1 Tbs. cooking oil	⅛ tsp. powdered sage or thyme
1 lb. mixed chopped beef, veal, and pork	pinch of cayenne
2 slices crustless whole-wheat bread soaked in ½ cup skim milk	1 cup vegetable water, stock, tomato juice, or stale beer for basting

Prepare kidneys (page 50), sprinkle with vinegar, and let stand in refrigerator. Glaze onions and green pepper in oil. Add mixed chopped meats, and brown, breaking with a fork as meat cooks. Put kidneys through medium blade of meat grinder and mix with browned meat, soaked bread, wheat germ, egg, and seasonings. Blend well. Form into loaf and put in center of lightly greased baking dish. Bake at 350° for 1 hour, basting occasionally with liquid. *Serves 6 to 8.*

Kidney Creole

1 lb. beef, veal, pork, or lamb kidneys	½ cup chopped green peppers
1 Tbs. vinegar	½ tsp. salt
3 Tbs. whole-wheat flour	¼ tsp. black pepper
3 slices bacon, chopped	1 small garlic clove, finely minced
½ cup chopped onions	1½ cups stewed tomatoes
	½ cup tomato juice or purée

Prepare kidneys (page 50), dice, and sprinkle with vinegar. Let stand for 1 hour in refrigerator. Roll diced kidneys in flour. Fry chopped bacon until almost crisp and drain off drippings. Add diced kidney, chopped vegetables, and seasonings. Stir well and sauté for 5

minutes. Add canned tomatoes and juice, and simmer for 10 minutes. Serve on brown or enriched rice, enriched noodles, or whole-wheat toast or biscuits (page 60). *Serves 4 to 6.*

Curried Kidneys

1 lb. veal or lamb kidneys	2 Tbs. butter or margarine, melted
1 Tbs. vinegar	½ tsp. salt
½ tsp. salt	dash of cayenne
sprinkling of black pepper	1 cup warm milk
2 Tbs. oil or bacon drippings	2 Tbs. skim-milk solids
2 Tbs. unbleached flour	
2–4 tsp. curry powder (depending on how much you like curry)	

Prepare kidneys (page 50), dice, and sprinkle with vinegar. Let stand for 1 hour in refrigerator. Season kidneys with salt and pepper, and brown in oil or bacon drippings for 3 minutes, stirring often. Remove from heat while you make curry sauce: Mix flour and curry powder; blend with melted butter or margarine in top of double boiler to a smooth paste. Add seasonings. Mix warm milk with milk solids and add slowly, stirring until smooth and thickened. Add diced kidneys and heat without boiling. *Serves 4 to 6.*

Lamb Kidneys Gourmet

1 lb. lamb kidneys	½ cup beef stock
1 Tbs. vinegar	½ cup stewed tomatoes or tomato purée
salt and pepper	
2 Tbs. cooking oil	
3 Tbs. butter	2 Tbs. dry white wine (sherry or Madeira—for a gamy taste, use Marsala)
1 lb. sliced mushrooms	
1 Tbs. chopped chives or onion	
3 ozs. dry red wine (Burgundy, claret, etc.)	

Prepare kidneys (page 50) and cut again, into quarters. Sprinkle with vinegar, season with salt and pepper, and sauté in oil for 2 or 3 minutes, turning frequently until golden brown. Remove from pan and drain on paper towels. Discard oil from pan, wipe with paper towel, melt 2 tablespoons of the butter, and sauté mushrooms for 2 minutes. Add chopped chives or onion and red wine. Cook over low heat until half of the wine evaporates. Add beef stock and tomatoes, and heat. Below boiling point, swirl remaining tablespoon of butter and white wine into sauce. Return kidneys to pan; bring sauce to boiling point. Serve with a sprinkling of chopped parsley. *Serves 4.*

Kidney Sausage Bake with Brown Rice

1 lb. beef, veal, or lamb kidneys	2 small onions
1 Tbs. vinegar	1 small garlic clove, minced
½ cup uncooked brown rice	2 Tbs. chopped parsley
4 cups vegetable water	⅛ tsp. powdered sage
½ lb. pork sausage meat	2 Tbs. whole-wheat flour
1 large or 2 small carrots	1 Tbs. yeast flakes or brewers' yeast

Prepare kidneys (page 50), sprinkle with vinegar, dice, and let stand in refrigerator while you prepare rice. Soak rice for 1 hour in vegetable water; then cook it in the same water for 1 hour. Drain, reserving both rice and water. Cook sausage meat slowly over low heat, adding no grease, until enough fat has accumulated in the pan to sauté kidneys. Remove and reserve sausage meat and brown the kidneys for 3 minutes, stirring frequently. Reserve pan liquid. Put kidneys, sausage meat, and vegetables through meat grinder. Mix with parsley and sage. Put cooked rice in lightly greased baking dish, cover with meat mixture, and bake at 350° for 30 minutes. Add flour and yeast to pan liquid, stir until smooth, and add 1 cup of the water in which rice was cooked. Stir until hot and thickened and serve over meat and rice. *Serves 6 to 8.*

Liver

Please remember that other meat animals besides calves have livers. Calf's liver is very nice, and it provides generous amounts of the vitamins, minerals, and protein for which it is rightly acclaimed. However, the livers of other animals are likely to contain *more* of these essential nutrients per serving—usually because other animals have been permitted to live longer and therefore have had more time to accumulate and store in this vital organ of their bodies the life-preserving, healing, blood-building, health-giving elements it is the liver's function to accumulate and store.

Liver Fricassee

1 lb. beef, calf, pork, or lamb liver, sliced	2 cups canned tomatoes
½ tsp. salt	2 medium green peppers, chopped
⅛ tsp. pepper	½ cup sliced onions
¼ cup whole-wheat flour	½ tsp. celery salt
¼ cup bacon drippings or cooking oil	½ tsp. poultry seasoning

Dredge liver with seasoned flour and brown on both sides in bacon drippings or oil. Add tomatoes, peppers, onions, and seasonings. Cover and simmer for 30 minutes. (Serve with brown rice.) *Serves 4 to 6.*

Liver Paprika

½ cup chopped onions	salt and pepper to taste
3 Tbs. butter, margarine, or cooking oil	3 egg yolks, lightly beaten
1 lb. beef, calf, pork, or lamb liver	1 cup warm sour cream
1 heaping tsp. paprika	

Sauté onions in butter until golden. Dice and add liver, and stir in seasonings. Cook over low heat with frequent stirrings until just fork-tender—from 3 to 10 minutes, depending on which kind of liver you are using. Beat eggs into warm sour cream and stir over low heat to bubbling point. Do not boil. Combine with liver and onions. *Serves 4 to 6.*

Liver Casserole No. 1

1 lb. beef, calf, pork, or lamb liver	½ cup sliced stuffed olives
2 cups boiling vegetable water	1 tsp. salt
2 Tbs. butter or margarine	¼ tsp. paprika
2 Tbs. unbleached or whole-wheat flour	1 Tbs. Worcestershire sauce
2 Tbs. thinly sliced green celery	½ cup wheat germ
	2 hard-cooked eggs, chopped

Drop liver into boiling vegetable water, lower heat, and simmer for 5 minutes. Drain (reserve liquid) and cut into small dice. Melt butter and blend with flour to a smooth paste. Gradually add 1½ cups of water in which liver was simmered, stirring until sauce is smooth and thickened. Add liver, celery, olives, and seasonings. Pour into lightly greased casserole, sprinkle wheat germ over top, and bake, uncovered, at 350° for 20 minutes. Garnish with chopped hard-cooked eggs. *Serves 4 to 6.*

Liver Casserole No. 2

½ cup fine whole-wheat bread crumbs	1 cup chopped onions
½ cup wheat germ	⅔ cup chopped green celery with leaves
½ tsp. poultry seasoning	2 Tbs. bacon drippings or cooking oil
2 Tbs. finely chopped parsley	1 cup seasoned stock, vegetable water, or bouillon
1 lb. beef, pork, or lamb liver	1 Tbs. butter
1 Tbs. lemon juice	

Mix bread crumbs, wheat germ, poultry seasoning, and parsley and place half of this mixture in a well-greased casserole. Slice liver very thin and spread over crumb mixture. Sprinkle with lemon juice and let stand while you sauté onions and celery in bacon drippings or cooking oil until onions are glazed. Drain these vegetables and spread them over the liver. Pour seasoned stock over these ingredients, top with remaining crumb mixture, and dot with butter. Bake at 350° for 1 hour. *Serves 4 to 6.*

Deviled Liver

1½–2 lbs. beef, pork, or lamb liver	2 tsp. dry mustard
½ cup unbleached or whole-wheat flour	1 tsp. salt
3 onions, sliced	⅛ tsp. pepper
2 Tbs. bacon drippings or cooking oil	½ cup stock or vegetable water
	½ cup warm sour cream

Cut liver into small pieces and dredge with flour. Sauté onions in bacon drippings or oil until glazed. Add floured liver, and brown, turning, until tender and cooked through. Stir

seasonings into stock and add to pan. Bring to boiling point, stirring constantly. Reduce heat to below boiling point, stir in sour cream, and heat to serving temperature without boiling. *Serves 4 to 6.*

Liverburgers

1 lb. beef, pork, or lamb liver	⅛ tsp. pepper
2 small onions	2 Tbs. wheat germ
⅔ tsp. salt	1 egg, lightly beaten
	2 Tbs. cooking oil

Put liver and onions through medium blade of meat grinder. Mix with seasonings, wheat germ, and lightly beaten egg. Form into patties and brown on both sides in cooking oil—or pan-broil without oil for 2 minutes on each side. Serve on toasted whole-wheat or wheat-germ biscuits (page 60). Top with tomato slices. *Makes 4 to 6 patties.*

Vitamin B Protein Loaf

1 lb. pork liver	1 Tbs. chopped green celery
1 lb. lean pork	
2 eggs, lightly beaten	¼ tsp. black pepper
½ cup soft whole-wheat bread crumbs	⅛ tsp. each sage and thyme
½ cup wheat germ	1 large clove garlic, minced or pressed
1½ tsp. salt	
1 Tbs. chopped parsley	

Put liver and pork through fine blade of your meat grinder. Combine with all other ingredients. Form into a loaf, or press into a baking dish, and set dish in a shallow pan of hot water. Bake at 300° for 2 hours. *Serves 4 to 6, with leftovers for cold sandwiches.*

Liver Dumplings

These may be used to hearten further a hearty soup such as tomato, pea, or lentil—or as a satisfying luncheon or supper course.

1 lb. beef, pork, or lamb liver	1½ cups soft whole-wheat bread crumbs
2 small onions	
1 tsp. salt	½ cup wheat germ
⅛ tsp. pepper	1½ Tbs. butter or margarine, melted—or bacon drippings
pinch of basil, oregano, or marjoram	

1 qt. boiling
vegetable water
(or soup)

2 eggs, lightly
beaten

Put liver and onions through fine blade of your meat grinder. Add all other ingredients and blend thoroughly. Drop by the tablespoonful into boiling vegetable water or soup, lower heat, cover, and simmer for 15 minutes. *Serves 4 to 6.*

Liver in Sweet and Sour Sauce

4 large, thin slices of
beef liver
4 Tbs. unbleached or
whole-wheat flour
1 egg, beaten
4 Tbs. wheat germ

4 Tbs. butter,
margarine, or
cooking oil
4 tsp. honey
4 tsp. lemon juice

Dredge liver slices in flour, dip in beaten egg, and roll in wheat germ. Brown on both sides in 3 tablespoons of shortening—about 3 or 4 minutes per side. Remove to heated serving dish and keep warm. Add remaining tablespoon of butter and the honey to skillet, and heat thoroughly but do not boil. Remove pan from heat, add lemon juice, and mix well. Return liver to skillet over low heat, and turn in the sweet and sour sauce until the slices are well coated on both sides. *Serves 4.*

Mexican Liver

1½ lbs. beef, pork, or
lamb liver, thinly
sliced
¼ cup bacon
drippings
2 large onions,
sliced
4 tomatoes, diced

2 cups vegetable
water or stock
2 tsp. chili powder
1 tsp. salt
pinch of black pepper
or cayenne
¼ tsp. curry powder

Brown liver slices on both sides in hot drippings. Remove from heat, drain on paper towel, and cut into ½-inch strips. Return liver to pan and add all other ingredients. Stir to mix well. Cover and simmer over low heat for 30 minutes. *Serves 4 to 6.*

Note: If fresh tomatoes are not available, use 1½ cups of stewed tomatoes and only 1 cup of vegetable water or stock.

Chicken Livers*

People who absolutely refuse to eat organ meats usually make an exception of chicken livers—possibly because of their delicate taste and texture, possibly because their higher cost puts them in the luxury class.

Nutritionally, chicken livers are not quite so desirable as the other varieties, but they are nevertheless quite good. So if chicken liver is the only liver your family will eat, I suggest you serve it as often as the budget permits.

Chicken livers are delicious sautéed very briefly in a little chicken fat or butter until they are just cooked through—a matter of 2 or 3 minutes. They may be scrambled with eggs, used in omelets, substituted for chicken in à la king recipes. (See chicken liver variation of Beef Stroganoff, page 46.)

Because very little "doctoring" is necessary to make chicken livers acceptable to family palates, only a handful of fancy recipes is given here, chosen chiefly for their accompanying ingredients which are rich in the high-quality proteins which non-organ-meat eaters may lack in their customary diets.

Several of the recipes to follow are especially recommended for the elderly, who as a class get all too little protein. These dishes are easy to chew and digest, are full of good nutrition—and their tastiness tempts lagging appetites.

Chicken Livers Paprika

1 large onion,
chopped
2 Tbs. melted chicken
fat, butter, or
margarine
¾–1 lb. chicken livers

1 heaping tsp.
paprika
salt to taste
1 cup sour cream
3 egg yolks

Glaze onions in melted fat or butter. Add chicken livers and seasonings, and stir over low heat for 5 minutes, turning the livers often. In a separate saucepan scald sour cream

Much commercial chicken production is accelerated by the use of arsenic compounds. The use of such feeds is supposed to be stopped well before the fowl are slaughtered, but FDA inspections indicate the rule is frequently ignored, with the result that commercial chicken liver may contain undesirable amounts of arsenic. If you can find organically raised fowl—which some health food stores stock—the extra cost may be well justified.

and beat in egg yolks. Continue to beat over low heat until mixture begins to bubble. Combine with liver-onion mixture. Serve over brown rice cooked in chicken stock or consommé, or on whole-wheat toast. *Serves 4 to 6*.

Chicken Livers with Apples

1 lb. chicken livers	4 Tbs. butter or
4 Tbs. whole-wheat	margarine, melted
flour	3 or 4 firm apples
1 tsp. salt	1 Tbs. brown sugar
½ tsp. paprika	

Dredge livers in mixture of flour, salt, and paprika and sauté in 2 tablespoons of the melted butter, turning to brown both sides evenly. Remove from pan; add remaining 2 tablespoons of butter. Wash and core apples; then slice them thickly (about ½-inch slices). Dredge apple slices with brown sugar and sauté in melted butter until tender, turning to glaze both sides. *Serves 4*.

Note: This recipe is also good with the addition of ½ cup sliced glazed onions.

Sweetbreads

I sometimes wonder whether it is semantics, relative scarcity, or high price which accounts for sweetbreads' place on fashionable menus which never include brains. If sweetbreads were called by their physiological name—thymus glands—would they be as desirable? On the other hand, if brains were given a more poetic and concealing name, would they suddenly become popular? Sweetbreads' delicacy, texture, and flavor are greatly appealing to many a person who wouldn't dream of lifting a forkful of brains—whose delicacy, texture, and flavor are so similar as to be undistinguishable in most recipes.

To Prepare Sweetbreads for Recipes

Wash quickly under running cold water and remove connective membranes.

Or: Barely cover with lightly salted water to which you have added 1 tablespoon of vinegar. Simmer gently for 15 minutes. Cool, and remove membranes. Simmering makes it a little easier to handle the sweetbreads, but a percentage of their nutrients is now in the water—so save it to use in stocks, soups, stews, and other recipes calling for water.

Creamed Sweetbreads

1 lb. sweetbreads	1 cup sweetbread
3 Tbs. butter or	stock
margarine, melted	salt and pepper to
3 Tbs. unbleached	taste
flour	(sherry)
1 cup warm milk	
¼ cup skim-milk	
solids	

Simmer sweetbreads (see above) and separate into small pieces, reserving 1 cup of the water. Blend butter and flour in saucepan until smooth, and add warm milk, milk solids, and sweetbread stock, stirring to prevent lumps. Season to taste and add sweetbreads. If you like, add 1 or 2 teaspoons of sherry for each adult serving. Serve on whole-wheat toast or wheat-germ biscuits (page 60). *Serves 4 to 6*.

Breaded Sweetbreads

1 lb. sweetbreads	½ tsp. salt
1 egg, beaten with 1	⅛ tsp. pepper
Tbs. milk (or cooled	2 Tbs. butter or
sweetbread stock)	margarine, melted
½ cup wheat germ or	
fine whole-wheat	
bread crumbs	

Separate washed or simmered (see above) sweetbreads into 4 serving pieces. Roll in egg mixture and wheat germ or bread crumbs seasoned with salt and pepper. Brown in hot butter or margarine. *Serves 4*.

Sweetbread Scallop

1 lb. sweetbreads	¼ cup chopped green
½ lb. mushrooms,	celery
sliced	1 Tbs. chopped
¼ cup chopped onions	parsley
2 Tbs. butter or	salt and pepper
margarine, melted	(paprika) to taste
2 Tbs. unbleached	3 Tbs. wheat germ
flour	1 Tbs. grated yellow
½ cup sour cream	cheese
2 cups stock or	
vegetable water (1	
cup may be	
sweetbread stock)	

Simmer sweetbreads as described, drain, and reserve stock. Sauté mushrooms and onions in butter or margarine for 3 minutes. Sprinkle flour over them and cook over low heat, stirring, for 3 minutes more. Heat sour cream and stock, and add to pan, stirring briskly to prevent lumps. When sauce is smooth, add celery and parsley, and season to taste. Simmer sauce for 10 minutes, stirring occasionally; then add sweetbreads and mix well. Transfer to a lightly greased baking dish and sprinkle with wheat germ and cheese. Bake at 350° for 20 minutes. *Serves 4.*

Note: This recipe can be extended to serve 6 or more by adding diced cooked chicken, turkey, or veal—1 or more cups. Add and fold into the sweetbread mixture just before it is transferred to the baking dish.

Note also: If your family loves sweetbreads but not brains, try combining the two for this recipe.

Sweetbread Kabobs

1 lb. sweetbreads	8–12 large stuffed
8–12 slices of bacon	olives
8–12 fairly large	1 Tbs. oil or melted
mushroom caps	butter

Prepare sweetbreads (page 55) and separate into pieces about the size of large walnuts. Wrap each piece with a strip of bacon. Thread wrapped sweetbreads, mushrooms, and olives on skewers and sauté, turning often, in large skillet or on a griddle—for about 5 minutes. When bacon begins to melt and become transparent, transfer the kabobs to the broiler, arranging the skewers across the top of an empty metal bread or cake pan. Broil, turning from time to time, until bacon is crisp. *Serves 4 to 6.*

Tongue

All animals have edible tongues. The pampered princesses of fairy tales dined delicately on hummingbirds' tongues, and very possibly some of the gourmet food shops still stock them along with the fried baby bees, sautéed grasshoppers, smoked rattlesnake meat, and marinated ants they provide for the limited but enthusiastic audience which dotes on spooky foods. More practical sizes of tongues are available for main meat courses, but they are neglected far too much except in enlightened households, especially those with European backgrounds. Here again, as with brains and sometimes kidneys, the objection to tongue seems to be a matter of philosophy rather than taste. Few dishes are as delicious as well-prepared tongue.

Tongue is not properly an organ meat. It is, rather, a well-exercised muscle which means that it requires longer cooking for tenderness. Remember the lesson repeated throughout this book that long cooking in water liberates essential vitamins and minerals. When you cook tongue for the sake of its taste as well as its excellent protein, make it a habit to save part of the cooking water as the basis of dried legume soups or to add to stews.

Simmered Tongue, Fresh or Smoked

1 fresh or smoked	1 bay leaf
beef tongue—or 2	3 or 4 cloves
veal, or 8 lamb	1 tsp. peppercorns
tongues	1 onion, sliced
water to cover	a few celery tops with
(1 tsp. salt per qt. of	leaves—or 1 Tbs.
water for fresh	celery flakes
tongue only; omit	
salt for smoked	
tongue)	

Special note for smoked tongue: Depending on the type you purchase, smoked tongue may or may not require soaking in cold water for 3 hours or more to remove some of the saltiness. If no soaking is required, the label on its wrapping will say so. If there is no label—soak it.

Cover tongue with water, add all other ingredients, and bring to boiling point; then lower heat and simmer, covered, until tender. You'll find that from 50 to 60 minutes per pound of beef tongue will do it—somewhat less for smaller ones. To be sure, stick a fork into the tip end. If this is tender, so is the rest. Let tongue cool in the cooking water. When it can be handled, remove the skin and roots, which can be used to add flavor to legume soups. See recipes at the end of this section for sauces. *Serves 6 to 8.*

Honeyed Tongue

1 fresh beef tongue	2 tsp. whole cloves
½ cup honey	stuck into slices of
½ cup brown sugar	½ lemon
1 cup stewed fruit or	(slices of ½ lemon)
berries—any kind	

Simmer tongue (see above). Blend all remaining ingredients with 1 cup of liquid reserved from cooking water, and simmer the tongue in this mixture for 15 minutes. Slice tongue and serve with its own sauce. Garnish with cloved lemon slices. *Serves 6 to 8.*

Cold Jellied Beef Tongue with Raw Vegetables

1 smoked beef tongue	½ cup shredded carrots
3 cups of water in which tongue is cooked	½ cup chopped green peppers
1½ Tbs. unflavored gelatin	½ cup shredded cabbage
¼ cup lemon juice	½ cup raisins
1 Tbs. brown sugar	2 or 3 hard-cooked eggs
1 cup chopped green celery	fresh parsley

Simmer tongue (page 56). Dip out ½ cup of the tongue liquid and cool in refrigerator. Measure 2½ cups more of the liquid and simmer. Stir 1½ tablespoons unflavored gelatin into the cold tongue liquid, and add this to the simmering tongue liquid. (You may add 2 beef or chicken bouillon cubes, or 1 cube and 1 teaspoonful of Worcestershire sauce, if you like.) Stir in lemon juice and sugar, and remove from heat. Remove to refrigerator until mixture thickens. Stir in vegetables and raisins. Moisten an aspic mold or bread pan with cold water and cover the bottom with a few spoonfuls of the gelatin mixture. Add a layer of sliced hard-cooked egg. Place the trimmed tongue on this and cover with the rest of the gelatin mixture. Chill thoroughly in the refrigerator. Turn upside down on a bed of lettuce to unmold, and garnish with remainder of hard-cooked eggs and with parsley. *Serves 6 to 8.*

Sauces for Fresh or Smoked Tongue

Sour Cream and Horseradish Sauce

1 firm, tart apple	½ tsp. grated lemon or orange peel
1½ cups sour cream	⅛ tsp. paprika
½ cup white horseradish	dash of cayenne
1 tsp. brown sugar	

Peel apple and grate it immediately into sour cream. Add remaining ingredients and blend thoroughly. This may be served cold, or heated through without boiling.

Vegetable Sauce

3 Tbs. unbleached or whole-wheat flour	1 cup diced or shredded carrots
1 Tbs. yeast flakes or brewers' yeast	½ cup chopped onions
1½ cups liquid in which tongue was cooked	½ cup diced green celery
	½ tsp. salt
	¼ tsp. pepper

Make a smooth paste of flour, yeast, and a little of the tongue water. Add remaining liquid gradually, stirring to prevent lumps. Add vegetables and seasonings, and simmer until vegetables are tender.

Curry Sauce

3 Tbs. butter or margarine, melted	1 tsp. onion juice or minced onion
3 Tbs. unbleached flour	1–2 tsp. curry powder
1 cup water in which tongue was cooked	1 tsp. lemon juice
1 cup milk or skim milk	salt, pepper, and paprika to taste

Blend melted butter and flour to a smooth paste. Gradually add warm tongue liquid and milk, and stir to prevent lumps. Cook over low heat until sauce begins to thicken; then stir in remaining ingredients.

Mustard Sauce

3 Tbs. butter or margarine, melted	1 cup milk or skim milk
3 Tbs. unbleached flour	1–2 Tbs. table mustard
1 cup tongue liquid	salt to taste

Blend butter and flour to a smooth paste. Gradually add warm tongue liquid and milk, and stir to prevent lumps. Cook over low heat until sauce begins to thicken. Stir in mustard and salt (if needed).

8
The Staff of Life

On the modern American scene, much if not most of that which poses as bread is a tribute to engineering ingenuity, advertising cleverness, and packaging artistry. It is also an insult to human intelligence.

The Egyptians are credited with having invented bread, as we know it. That was back in the time of the ancient Pharaohs, several thousands of years B.C. Ever since then, it seems, there has been a conspiracy afoot to see just how much nutrition could be taken out of bread and still have people willing to buy and eat it. That this conspiracy was brilliantly successful is implicit in recent government action which enjoins bakers and millers to put back into bread and flour some of the nutrients they remove. Note, I said "some." According to the best of calculations, about four times more vital nutrients are removed from wheat processed into white bread flour than are replaced in the current "enrichment" program. This makes about the same kind of sense as rice refinement, which polishes off the grain's true nutrients. The pretty white rice is sold to people and the polishings to the vitamin industry. The vitamin industry sells supplements made from rice polishings to people who need them because they've been eating white rice.

Most commercial flour used by the bakeries or at home is beautiful to behold and scrupulously sanitary. It's as white as snow, as fine as silk, as pure as a sterile hospital gown—and approximately as nourishing.

There was a time when the flour milled from wheat contained all of wheat's goodness—its protein, enzymes, amino acids, vitamins, and minerals. Modern milling processes have almost entirely done away with most of wheat's truest nutrient value—its germ. If you could examine a single grain of wheat under a microscope, cutting it into thin slices to show a cross section, you would see a demonstration of nature's way of concentrating life in a speck. The outer skin is familiar to you as bran. It is made up of a fibrous carbohydrate substance we call cellulose, and it contains a few minerals and vitamins as well. The bran, valuable in diet as roughage, accounts for about 14 percent of the grain.

Working toward the center, the next mass visible in the cross section is the kernel, called endosperm or middlings, and it is composed of starch and a little gluten. Gluten, a protein, holds bread dough together when you add water and yeast. The kernel is the bulkiest part of the grain—85 percent of it.

Thus far, the microscope reveals, we have 14 percent bran and 85 percent carbohydrate kernel in a grain of wheat. What about the remaining 1 percent? This is the germ or embryo, the heart of wheat, the reservoir for vastly important vitamins, unsaturated fatty acids, and other vital nutrients.

Wheat germ contains protein, unsaturated fat, thiamin, niacin, and most of the other B Complex vitamins. It also contains precursors of arachidonic acid, a type of fatty acid important to the functioning of the brain. In wheat-germ oil is a 25-carbon waxy alcohol, used for such degenerative disorders as multiple sclerosis. It is also the richest natural source of a vitamin largely removed from our carbohydrate foods: Vitamin E, which—contrary to popular thinking—is more important to slowing down aging than it is in reproduction.

In almost all store-bought white bread, the wheat germ has been ruthlessly sacrificed on the altar of modern milling processes because of certain problems raised by storage and transportation. Wheat germ, containing the oil-soluble vitamin E, becomes rancid if stored too long. Moreover, it attracts mice and other vermin who won't bother with refined flour if they can help it because they know instinctively it is not nourishing enough to ensure natural life span, freedom from disease, and continuation of their species.

If you look for it in the right places, it is possible to buy 100 percent whole-wheat bread with the wheat germ intact. Similarly, it is possible to buy 100 percent whole-wheat or whole-rye flour for home baking, and unbleached white flour which has escaped at least some of the superrefining of most commercial flours or which has had wheat germ restored to it.

Also available in modest mills springing up all over the countryside in response to mounting interest in good nutrition are cracked wheat, graham, peanut, potato, rice, bean, cottonseed, flaxseed, and soybean flours, along with whole-cereal grains.

If you are, as I hope, in a mood to embark on a bake-your-own-bread program for good nutrition, it is worthwhile looking into some of these sources for carefully milled flours and grains. They are likely to be somewhat more expensive than ordinary commercial grades, unfortunately, because they are produced in lesser quantities and by small mills rather than by the big combines. Moreover, because of widespread faddism which labels some foods as "health foods" and sells them in "health food stores," the prices of natural grains and flours from these sources are too often inflated beyond justice.

In the pages to follow, you will find a few recipes calling for some of these less easily obtained flours and grains. However, I face the reality that time, budget considerations, convenience, and the line of least resistance will inevitably lead all except the most zealous to the supermarket shelves. Therefore, the greatest number of recipes given here make the best of the more readily available whole wheat, unbleached, and vitamin-enriched flour in the happy knowledge that there are also readily available wheat germ, brewers' yeast, yeast flakes, and skim-milk solids to permit your bread to emerge from the oven with considerably more virtue than most of the stuff you're used to.

Using Commercial Mixes

The best advice in buying commercial biscuit and cake mixes is: don't. In bygone years, one could in good conscience tell the hard-pressed housewife how to improve the nutritional value (and the palatability) of these concoctions, by using wheat germ, soy flour, and non-fat milk. Now their labels read like prescriptions, and there are no nutritious additions that offset the undesirability of preservatives like BHA and BHT, or artificial flavors and colors. BHT has been found to have so profound an impact on the animal brain and animal behavior that a leading American University asked FDA to ban these chemicals from use as food additives. If you can locate mixes which are innocent of such chemicals, you can improve them nutritionally by the addition of nutritious yeast—1 teaspoonful per cup, and wheat germ in the same quantity. Even then, you are still serving less nutritious food than your own baked recipes, made with yeast, for yeast recipes are always superior to those made with baking powder.

Good-Nutrition Biscuits

Baking Powder Biscuits

Wheat-Germ Biscuits

2½ cups whole-wheat or unbleached flour	1 cup wheat germ
1 tsp. salt	3 Tbs. chilled solid shortening, lard,
2½ tsp. double-acting baking powder	margarine, or bacon grease
¼ cup skim-milk solids	¾ cup milk

Mix all dry ingredients together. Cut in shortening with pastry blender or two knives until mixture is coarsely granular. Add milk all at once and stir with a fork until moistened. Turn out on a floured board or waxed paper and knead lightly until fairly smooth. Pat or roll out to ¾ inch thickness and cut with floured biscuit cutter. Place on greased baking sheet and bake at 425° for 15 to 18 minutes. *Makes 16.*

Dropped Biscuits

Increase the milk by an additional ¼ cup. Drop by the spoonful onto greased baking sheet or into greased muffin tins.

Sour Cream or Sour Milk Biscuits

Substitute sour cream or sour milk for fresh for either of the preceding methods.

Vitamin C Biscuits

For the liquid, use half milk and half fruit juice—orange, pineapple, apricot, apple—anything you happen to have open, even tomato juice, whose vitamin C is protected in cooking by the natural acidity of tomatoes.

Bran Biscuits

1 cup whole-wheat, unbleached, or enriched flour	2½ tsp. double-acting baking powder
1 cup whole bran—or ½ cup each whole bran and wheat germ	4 Tbs. chilled solid shortening, lard, margarine, or bacon grease
½ tsp. salt	½ cup milk
¼ cup skim-milk solids	

Mix all dry ingredients together. Cut in shortening with pastry blender or two knives.

Add milk and stir with a fork. Dough will be soft. Pat it on waxed paper to ½ inch thickness, cut with floured biscuit cutter, and place on greased cookie sheet—or add a little more milk and drop by the spoonful onto sheet or into greased muffin tins. Bake at 425° for 15 to 18 minutes. *Makes 16.*

Cheese Biscuits

2 cups sifted enriched, unbleached, or whole-wheat flour	1 cup grated sharp yellow cheese
2½ tsp. double-acting baking powder	4 Tbs. solid shortening, lard, margarine, or bacon grease
¾ tsp. salt	¾ cup milk

Mix all dry ingredients together, including cheese. Cut in shortening with pastry blender or two knives. Add milk and stir with fork until well blended. Turn out onto lightly floured board or waxed paper and knead lightly. Pat or roll dough to ½ inch thickness, cut with floured biscuit cutter, and place on greased cookie sheet. Or—add ¼ cup more milk, mix well with dry ingredients, and drop by the spoonful onto sheet or into greased muffin tins. Bake at 450° for 12 to 15 minutes. *Makes 16.*

Peanut Butter Biscuits

2 cups whole-wheat or unbleached flour	1 Tbs. brewers' yeast or yeast flakes
¾ tsp. salt (less, if peanut butter is very salty)	3 Tbs. butter or margarine
¼ cup skim-milk solids	4 Tbs. peanut butter
3 tsp. double-acting baking powder	1 cup milk
	1 Tbs. dark molasses or honey

Mix dry ingredients together. Cream butter or margarine with peanut butter; then cut this blend into the dry ingredients with a pastry blender or two knives. Add milk and molasses (or honey), and mix briskly with a fork. Drop by the spoonful onto greased cookie sheet or into greased muffin tins. Bake at 450° for 15 minutes. *Makes 12 to 15.*

Shortcake Biscuits

1¾ cups sifted unbleached or enriched flour	2½ tsp. double-acting baking powder
	1 tsp. salt

¼ cup skim-milk	1 Tbs. honey
solids	2 Tbs. butter,
3 Tbs. chilled butter	melted
¾ cup cream (try	
sour cream)	

Resift flour with other dry ingredients. Cut in chilled butter with pastry blender or two knives. Add cream and honey and stir well with a fork. Turn out onto lightly floured board or waxed paper, and divide dough into 2 unequal parts—roughly, ⅔ and ⅓. Pat or roll larger quantity into desired shapes or cut with floured biscuit cutter; then brush with melted butter. These are the bottom halves of shortcakes. Pat or roll remaining dough into similar but thinner shapes, and cover bottom halves. Bake on greased cookie sheet at 450° for 12 to 15 minutes. When slightly cooled, these biscuits are easily separated into halves. *No quantity given:* These may be made small, for dainty desserts, or large, for family servings.

Soybean Biscuits

If you've never tasted soybean flour biscuits—or soybean anything, for that matter—it might be wise for you to start out with either of the lesser quantities of soybean flour and the corresponding greater quantity of regular flour given in the following recipe. Unlike the grain flours, soybean has a distinctive taste of its own. Many people like this taste, others do not. In the lesser quantities it is not pronounced, yet it still provides excellent high-quality proteins lacking in grain. If you find that you and your family like the taste, increase the quantity of soybean flour in future recipes, ending up cup for cup with wheat flour. In a protein-needy nation, the more you can get the better.

Soybean Biscuits

2 cups flour,	4, 3, or 2 Tbs. solid
comprising ¼, ½, or	shortening (more if
1 cup soybean flour	you are using less
and 1¾, 1½, or 1	soybean flour,
cup whole-wheat or	which has fat
unbleached flour	content)
2½ tsp. double-acting	⅔ cup skim-milk
baking powder	

Sift dry ingredients together, cut in shortening with pastry blender or two knives, and add

milk quickly. Mix well, and knead lightly on a floured board or waxed paper. Roll or pat to ½ inch thickness, place on greased cookie sheet, and bake at 425° for 15 to 20 minutes. *Makes 12 to 18, depending on size.*

Note: If you recognize the value of soybean flour's protein content and wish to use it in maximum quantities but are not crazy about the taste, try using peanut butter and shortening, half and half. Cream them together and cut into the dry ingredients.

Yeast Biscuits

Make either of these recipes when you're expecting a crowd, or if you own a freezer. The use of yeast means a little more time and work than you ordinarily care to devote to mere biscuits—but, then, these aren't mere. The yields are large to permit you to make an impression at a party, or to freeze however many the family doesn't consume at one sitting. Freeze biscuits wholly baked, when cool, in plastic bags. To serve, put them into a 400° oven without thawing and remove them when heated through.

Southern Raised Split Biscuits No. 1
Eggless, single-rising, made with dry yeast.

1 package dry yeast	¼ cup skim-milk
2 cups lukewarm	solids
milk, skim milk,	½ cup solid
or vegetable water	shortening or mar-
1 tsp. salt	garine—or ¼ cup
(about) 5 cups sifted	each of
enriched,	shortening and
unbleached, or	butter
whole-wheat flour	¼ cup butter or
1 Tbs. brown sugar	margarine, melted

Sprinkle yeast over lukewarm liquid and let it rest for 5 minutes while you sift dry ingredients together. Cut in the solid shortening with pastry blender or two knives. When thoroughly blended, add yeast-liquid solution and mix briskly with a fork until dough is soft. You may add a little more flour if necessary to make dough easy to handle. Turn out on floured board or waxed paper, and roll to ¼ inch thickness. Cut with floured cutter. Brush half the rounds with melted butter or margarine and top with the remainder. Place on greased cookie sheet, cover lightly with a clean cloth or towel, and let rise in a warm place (80 to 85°) for an hour or more, until double in bulk. Bake in (preheated) 425° oven for 10 to 12 minutes. *Makes 3 dozen.*

Southern Raised Split Biscuits No. 2

Triple-rising sponge method with eggs, potatoes, compressed yeast.

6 medium potatoes	(about) 11 cups
1 compressed yeast	enriched or
cake	unbleached flour
1 Tbs. brown sugar	(up to 5 cups of
2 cups lukewarm	total may be
milk, skim milk, or	whole-wheat)
vegetable water	½ cup skim-milk
½ cup solid	solids
shortening	2 Tbs. brewers' yeast
½ cup butter	½ cup butter or
2 eggs	margarine, melted
2 tsp. salt	

While potatoes are boiling in their jackets, crumble yeast and sugar over the lukewarm milk or other liquid. When potatoes are soft, peel and mash them fine while they are still hot. Add shortening and butter, and mash again. Beat eggs with salt and beat into the hot potatoes. Add and stir in the yeast-liquid mixture. Stir in enough of the flour to make a soft sponge—about 3 cups. Let the sponge rise in a warm place until double in bulk. Sift together the remaining flour, milk solids, and brewers' yeast, and work this mixture into the sponge until the dough is easily handled. Knead lightly in the bowl until smooth, form into a tight ball, cover with clean cloth or towel, and let rise again until double. Punch down, roll on floured board to ½ inch thickness, and cut with floured biscuit cutter. Brush tops of half of the rounds with melted butter or margarine, top with the remaining rounds, cover, and let rise again until double on greased cookie sheets. Bake at 400° for 15 minutes. *Makes 4 to 5 dozen.*

Muffins

If you can find commercial muffin mixes without the usual preservatives—and it is more of a possibility than with cake mixes—you can give them greater nutritional values by these steps:

When the box recipe calls for 1 cup of mix, add 1 or 2 teaspoons of wheat germ before filling the cup with mix.

When the box recipe calls for water, use vegetable cooking water.

When it calls for milk, put ⅛ cup of skim milk powder in a measuring cup, fill the cup with whole milk, and beat or blend until thoroughly dissolved.

Instead of sugar, use dark molasses or honey. With honey—which is not really more desirable than any other form of sugar—you will at least use less, for it is sweeter. The molasses at least gives a bit of iron and another useful nutrient.

But if you're going to be a c.g.n. cook (creative, good-nutrition) make your own muffins from scratch.

Good-Nutrition Plain Baking Powder Muffins

2 cups whole-wheat,	1¼ cups milk
unbleached, or	2 Tbs. butter or
enriched flour	margarine, melted
¼ cup wheat germ	2 Tbs. bacon
2½ tsp. double-acting	drippings or
baking powder	melted
½ tsp. salt	chicken fat
¼ cup skim-milk	2 Tbs. dark
solids	molasses or honey
1 egg	

Combine dry ingredients and mix well. Beat together the egg, milk, melted shortenings, and sweetener. Pour these into the dry ingredient mixture all at once and stir briskly until batter is moist. Don't overwork. The batter will have a lumpy appearance, and that's how it should be. Fill greased muffin tins about ⅔ full and bake at 425° for 25 minutes. *Makes 12 to 15.*

Better-Nutrition Plain Yeast Muffins

2 cakes compressed	2 Tbs. dark molasses
yeast—or 2	or honey
packages dry yeast	1 egg, lightly beaten
1 cup lukewarm	1 cup whole-wheat,
milk, buttermilk,	unbleached, or
or skim milk	enriched flour
2 Tbs. butter or	1 tsp. salt
margarine, melted	¼ cup skim-milk
2 Tbs. bacon	solids
drippings or	½ cup wheat germ
chicken fat	

Add yeast to warm milk and let stand for 10 minutes. Add shortenings, sweetener, and lightly beaten egg, and stir until well mixed. Sift together the flour, salt, and milk solids. Stir wheat germ into this mixture and add to the liquid. Stir briskly with a fork until moist and lumpy, and drop by the spoonful into greased muffin tins. These may be prepared an hour or so in advance of baking, if you wish them to rise. After they have doubled in bulk, bake at 425° for 15 minutes. Or—bake immediately at 350° for 20 minutes. *Makes 12 to 15.*

Special Note: Substituting Yeast for Baking Powder in Muffin Recipes

Most of the recipes which follow can be made with yeast instead of baking power—for better nutrition, and with very little extra trouble.

To make muffins with yeast: Omit baking powder. Use 1 or 2 cakes of compressed yeast, or 1 or 2 packages of dry yeast per recipe. Heat milk (or other liquid specified) to lukewarm and combine with yeast (and sweetener, if recipe calls for one). Let this mixture stand for 10 minutes. Combine remaining ingredients called for in recipe you are using and add to the yeast mixture. Stir briskly with a fork until mixture is moist and lumpy, and drop by the spoonful into greased muffin tins. Fill the cups to the half-way mark. You may let muffins rise in a warm place until double in bulk and then bake them at the oven temperature and baking time specified in the recipe; or—you may bake them immediately in a 350° oven, increasing the specified baking time by 5 to 10 minutes.

Oatmeal Muffins

1½ cups sifted unbleached, whole-wheat, or enriched flour	¼ cup skim-milk solids
⅓ cup oatmeal	2½ tsp. double-acting baking powder*
¼ cup wheat germ	1 egg, beaten
½ tsp. salt	1 cup milk
1 Tbs. brown sugar	3 Tbs. melted margarine or oil
1 Tbs. dark molasses or honey	

Combine all dry ingredients. Mix together the egg, milk, and melted shortening, and pour all at once into the dry ingredients. Stir briskly until moist but somewhat lumpy. Fill greased muffin tins ⅔ full and bake at 425° for 25 minutes. *Makes 12 to 15.*

*See note regarding yeast above.

Fruited Brown Rice Muffins

2¼ cups whole-wheat, unbleached, or enriched flour	3 tsp. double-acting baking powder*
¼ cup wheat germ	1 cup milk
1 tsp. salt	1 egg, beaten
¾ cup chopped pitted dates, seedless raisins, or chopped cooked prunes	¾ cup cooked brown rice
	2 Tbs. oil or melted shortening

Sift together flour, baking powder, and salt, and stir in wheat germ. Add fruit, milk, beaten egg, rice, and shortening, and blend briskly. Fill greased muffin tins ⅔ full and bake at 425° for 30 minutes. *Makes 15 to 18.*

Banana-Bran Muffins

1 cup sifted whole-wheat, unbleached, or enriched flour	3 Tbs. dark molasses
2 Tbs. skim-milk solids	2½ tsp. double-acting baking powder*
½ tsp. salt	¼ cup milk
1 cup whole bran	1 cup mashed ripe banana
1 egg, beaten	2 Tbs. oil or melted shortening

Sift together the flour, baking powder, milk solids, and salt. Stir in bran and distribute well. Combine egg, molasses, milk, banana, and shortening, and add all at once to dry ingredients. Stir briskly to blend. Fill greased muffin tins ⅔ full and bake at 400° for 20 to 25 minutes. *Makes 12 to 15.*

Fruit-Nut Banana Flake Muffins

½ cup enriched flour	3 Tbs. melted butter or margarine, or oil
½ cup whole-wheat flour	1 tsp. salt
⅓ cup skim-milk solids	2½ tsp. double-acting baking powder*
½ cup wheat germ	½ cup seedless raisins
1 cup milk or buttermilk	½ cup finely chopped or ground nut meats
2 Tbs. dark molasses, honey, or brown sugar	⅓ cup banana flakes
1 egg, beaten	

Sift together the flours, milk solids, salt, and baking powder. Add and stir in wheat germ. Combine milk, sweetener, egg, and melted shortening, and add to dry ingredients, stirring just enough to mix. Fold in the nut meats, raisins, and banana flakes, distributing well. Fill greased muffin tins ⅔ full and bake at 425° for 12 to 15 minutes. *Makes 12 to 15.*

Cup-for-Cup Cornmeal Muffins

1 cup undegerminated corn meal	1 egg, beaten
1 tsp. salt	1 cup whole-wheat, unbleached, or enriched flour
2 tsp. brown sugar	2½ tsp. double-acting baking powder*
2 Tbs. cooking oil	
1¼ cups milk	1 Tbs. brewers' yeast or yeast flakes
¼ cup skim-milk solids	

Put corn meal, salt, sugar, oil, and milk in top of double boiler, stir, and cook over boiling water for 10 minutes. Let cool. When cool, add beaten egg and stir. Sift together flour, baking powder, milk solids, and yeast, and stir into milk and cornmeal mixture. Fill greased muffin tins ⅔ full. Bake at 400° for 5 minutes, reduce heat to 350°, and bake 15 minutes more. *Makes 12 to 15.*

Cornmeal–Bacon Muffins

4 slices bacon	1 cup cold milk
2 cups undegerminated corn meal	2 eggs
	2½ tsp. double-acting baking powder
½ tsp. salt	
¼ cup skim-milk solids	2 Tbs. bacon drippings
2 cups boiling vegetable water	

Fry bacon crisp, drain, crumble, and reserve. Also reserve bacon drippings. Combine corn meal, salt, and milk solids in mixing bowl, and pour boiling vegetable water over the mixture. Immediately add cold milk; stir well to prevent lumps. Beat eggs into this mixture, add baking powder and bacon drippings, and blend well. Stir in crisp bacon bits. Pour into greased muffin tins and bake at 475° for 25 minutes. *Makes 15 to 18.*

Raised Griddle-Baked English Muffins
Caution: If English muffins are a favorite at your house, I advise you not to make these unless you resign yourself to repeating often.

See note regarding yeast, page 63.

Freezer owners can make up several batches at a time to store for a month or two of Sundays. They'll keep longer than that in the freezer (up to a year), but not if the family knows where to find them.

¾ cup milk	1 cake compressed yeast, or 1 package dry yeast*
½ cup water	
¼ cup warm water	
3 Tbs. shortening, melted (try chicken fat)	⅓ cup skim-milk solids
	1½ tsp. salt
1 egg, beaten	2 Tbs. butter or margarine, melted
1 Tbs. honey	
4 cups sifted whole-wheat, unbleached, or enriched flour	(about) ½ cup undegerminated cornmeal or wheat germ

Scald milk with ½ cup of water, remove from heat, and cool to lukewarm. Crumble or sprinkle yeast over ¼ cup warm water and let stand 10 minutes. When scalded milk is lukewarm, add the dissolved yeast, melted shortening, beaten egg, and honey. Resift flour with milk solids and salt. Combine dry and liquid ingredients, mixing to a soft dough. Turn out onto a floured board and knead for about 5 minutes, adding a little more flour if necessary to make handling easy. Dough should remain soft, however. Put dough in greased bowl, brush top with melted butter or margarine, cover with clean cloth, and let stand until double in bulk—about 1 hour. Roll out on floured board to about ⅓ inch thickness and let rest for 3 minutes. Cut with floured biscuit cutter, rekneading the scraps gently and rolling similarly. Pick muffins up carefully with pancake turner and place them on baking sheets or trays liberally covered with cornmeal or wheat germ. Sprinkle cornmeal or wheat germ on top of muffins. Let rise for 30 minutes. Heat ungreased griddle until drop of water bounces on it; then reduce heat to low. With pancake turner, carefully move muffins to griddle and bake over low heat for about 5 to 7 minutes. Turn and bake other side for same length of time. *Makes 15 to 20.*

Note: Unless you have a really first-class pretreated griddle, it might be wise to rub the griddle lightly with an oiled rag before each batch of muffins to prevent scorching.

For yeastier, faster muffins, use 2 cakes or packages of yeast. Reduce first rising time to 40 minutes, second rising to 20 minutes.

Bread

When you reach the point of baking your own bread for the sake of good nutrition, let's not have any nonsense about "quickie" loaves tossed together with one hand tied behind your back while the other hand measures out baking powder or baking soda. If speed is what you want, make biscuits. But if real, honest, body-and-soul-satisfying, praiseworthy *bread* is your goal, approach its creation as lovingly as an artist and be prepared to let it rise nobly and leisurely. For the most part you'll be working with yeast in the following recipes—or, rather, yeast will be working with you—and yeast insists on time in which to accomplish its leavening process.

Don't begrudge the time it takes to convert flour, liquid, shortening, and yeast into the aromatic poetry which emerges from your oven. Much of that time will not concern you directly. While the dough rests and rises you can be shopping, or doing chores, or watching television.

If you time your baking preparations strategically, you will have popped the loaf pans into the oven a half hour or so before your mate opens the front door to be greeted by the maddening perfume of hot, fresh, home-baked bread. This experience makes the term "breadwinner" less a cliché than an honorable title. (A nutritionist is not a marriage counselor, but I'm willing to bet that the ratio of divorces might just possibly drop in proportion to the number of households where home-baked bread is part of family enjoyment.)

Bread baking is neither mysterious nor difficult. Follow directions carefully. A few baking terms with which you should become familiar follow.

Baking Terms and Directions

Scald: Put cold liquid in a pan over moderate to high heat, and heat to just below the boiling point. When small bubbles appear around the edges where liquid meets pan, the proper scalding temperature has been reached.

Mix: Unless directions tell you to make a "sponge," which means to add only enough flour to form a loose, batterlike dough to which more flour will be added later, mixing requires you to use a rather large bowl in which you can begin to stir ingredients with a heavy spoon or fork. As they thicken, mix the ingredients by working them with your clean hands until well blended.

Knead: When dough is turned out on a floured board, it is likely to be a little sticky, clinging to your fingers and the board. Kneading means that you continually fold the dough over toward you, pressing down with the palms of your hands, turning it slightly, and folding and pressing again, until it becomes smooth and elastic.

Rise in a warm place: On warm summer days or evenings, just set the dough in a bowl on the counter in your warm kitchen. Yeast likes a temperature of from 80 to 85°. On cool or cold days, this temperature can be achieved by setting the bowl in your *unlighted* oven over a pan of hot (110°) water and closing the oven door. You may also place a covered bowl near a radiator or heat register.

Double in bulk: Yeast will usually cause dough to double its bulk in from 45 minutes to 2 hours, depending on how much yeast is used, its proportion to the other ingredients, and the warmth of the surroundings. Double or nearly double bulk is the size to aim for. Less will mean a heavy, unbread-like bread. More will mean a dry, coarse crumb because when yeast dough blows up beyond its desirable size it almost invariably deflates and falls down of its own accord. If you don't trust your eye to tell you when the dough has actually and accurately doubled, poke it in the center with your fingertips. If it is ready for the next step, it won't bounce back but will retain the imprint of your fingers.

Baking times are given in the recipes, but some ovens are "faster" than others. Bread is done when the loaf shrinks inward a little from the sides of the pan. When it is removed from the oven, remove it immediately from the pan and let it cool on a rack before slicing and eating.

Always preheat oven to indicated temperature before baking bread.

Good-Nutrition White Bread
Rising time about 2 hours. *Makes 3 loaves.*

3 cups whole or skim milk	2 cakes compressed yeast, or 2 packages' dry yeast
2 Tbs. honey	

6 cups sifted unbleached flour	3 Tbs. brewers' yeast
½ cup soybean flour or undegerminated corn meal	3 Tbs. wheat germ
	2 Tbs. liquid or melted shortening—oil, bacon drippings, chicken fat, butter, or margarine
¾ cup skim-milk solids	
4 tsp. salt	

Scald milk and cool to lukewarm. Crumble or sprinkle yeast over lukewarm milk, add honey, and let stand for 5 minutes. Resift flour with soybean flour, milk solids, salt, and brewers' yeast. Stir in wheat germ (and corn meal, if you are substituting this for soybean flour) and distribute well. Stir yeast-milk mixture, and, while stirring, add half of the flour mixture. Beat vigorously with rotary or electric beater until smoothly blended, add shortening, and beat again to mix well. Add remaining flour mixture, stirring first with a heavy spoon and then working with your hands. Turn dough out on a floured board and knead for about 5 minutes, until dough is smooth and elastic. (Use up to 1 cup more of unbleached flour if necessary.) Grease a large bowl, put dough in, and then turn dough upside down to grease all surfaces. Cover bowl with a slightly dampened clean cloth, and let dough rise in a warm place (80 to 85°) free of draughts until nearly double in size. This takes about 45 minutes, usually.

Punch dough down, fold edges in, and replace in bowl to rise 20 minutes more.

Turn out on a lightly floured board and divide dough into 3 equal parts. Fold each portion in toward its center to make smooth, tight balls. Cover with cloth and let rest on board for 10 minutes.

Shape 3 loaves to fit 3½- by 7½-inch tins and let rise in the tins until dough again doubles in size—about 45 minutes. Bake in preheated oven at 350° for a total of about 50 minutes. If loaves begin to brown within 15 or 20 minutes, reduce oven temperature to 325°. Remove from tins and put on rack or cloth to cool.

Good-Nutrition Yellow Bread

Rising time about 3 hours. *Makes 2 loaves.* (This is a substantial, compact, somewhat heavy bread—a stick-to-your ribs loaf especially good when toasted.)

1 cake compressed yeast or 1 package dry yeast	¼ cup warm vegetable water
	2 cups milk

3 Tbs. dark molasses or honey	2 eggs, lightly beaten
3 Tbs. brown sugar	1 cup undegerminated yellow corn meal
⅓ cup liquid or room-temperature shortening	
2½ tsp. salt	½ cup wheat germ
6 cups unbleached or enriched flour	

Crumble or sprinkle yeast over warm vegetable water and let stand for 5 minutes. Scald milk and combine with sweeteners, shortening, and salt. Mix well, and let cool to lukewarm. When lukewarm, add softened yeast, lightly beaten eggs, and 3 cups of the flour. Beat until smoothly blended with rotary or electric mixer. Add corn meal, wheat germ, and remaining flour, mixing first with a heavy spoon and then with your hands to make a soft dough.

Turn out on lightly floured board and knead for 10 minutes. Place in a greased bowl, turning once to grease all surfaces. Cover with slightly dampened clean cloth and let rise in a warm place until double in bulk—about 1½ to 2 hours. Punch down and let rest for 10 minutes. Divide dough in half and shape into 2 loaves. Place them in greased tins. Cover and let rise again until almost double—about 1 hour. Bake at 375° for 40 to 45 minutes.

100 Percent Whole-Wheat Bread

Rising time about 2 hours. *Makes 2 loaves.*

1 cake compressed yeast, or 1 package dry yeast	shortening (try bacon or ham grease or chicken fat)
½ cup lukewarm vegetable water	1 Tbs. salt
1 Tbs. brown sugar or honey	6 Tbs. dark molasses
2 cups milk or skim milk	5½ cups whole-wheat flour
2 Tbs. any oil or room-temperature	(½ cup wheat germ)

Crumble or sprinkle yeast over warm water; add honey and stir. Scald milk, remove from heat, and stir in shortening, salt, and dark molasses. Combine yeast water with milk mixture and beat with rotary or electric beater until well blended. Add liquid to flour (mixed with wheat germ), mix well, and knead in bowl for 2 or 3 minutes* (add a little vegetable water or milk if dough is stiff). Put dough in large greased bowl, turning once to grease all surfaces. Cover with a slightly dampened cloth and let rise until double in bulk—about 1 hour. Divide in equal parts without punching dough down, and form gently into 2 loaves which fit easily into greased bread pans. Cover and let rise again in warm place until double in bulk—about 1 hour. Preheat oven to 375° and bake for 20 minutes. Reduce heat to 325° and bake for 50 minutes to 1 hour, until bread shrinks away from sides of pans.

Wheat-Germ Bread

Rising time 2½ to 3 hours. *Makes 1 loaf.*

1 cup milk	yeast, or 1 pack-
1½ tsp. salt	age dry yeast
1 Tbs. brown sugar	(about) 3 cups sifted
1 Tbs. oil or melted	whole-wheat or
shortening	unbleached flour
1 cake compressed	1 cup wheat germ

Scald milk. Combine salt, sugar, and shortening and pour over these ingredients ¾ cup of the scalded milk. When remaining ¼ cup of scalded milk is lukewarm, crumble or sprinkle yeast over it and let stand. Combine 2½ cups of the flour with all of the wheat germ. Add dissolved yeast to milk mixture, beating with rotary or electric beater until thoroughly blended. Add to flour and mix thoroughly. Turn out onto board floured with remaining ½ cup of flour and knead for about 5 minutes, until dough is smooth and elastic. Put dough in greased bowl, turning to grease all surfaces. Cover with dampened cloth and let rise in a warm place until double in bulk. Knead again, lightly, on floured board. Cover (on board) with dampened cloth and let rise again until double in bulk. Punch down, shape into loaf, and put in greased bread tin. Cover and let rise again until double in bulk. Bake at 350° for 35 to 40 minutes.

Wheat-Germ French Bread (White or Whole-Wheat)

Rising time about 2 hours, 40 minutes. *Makes 2 loaves.*

1¼ cups vegetable water	1 Tbs. sugar

If you prefer a smoother grain, knead for 5 minutes. After first rising, punch down and knead again for 2 or 3 minutes before forming loaves.

1 cake compressed yeast, or 1 package dry yeast	2½ cups sifted enriched, unbleached, or whole-wheat flour
1½ tsp. salt	
1 tsp. softened shortening	1 cup wheat germ

Heat vegetable water to lukewarm. Crumble or sprinkle yeast over vegetable water and stir until dissolved. Stir in salt, shortening, and sugar. Combine flour with wheat germ and add liquid. Mix well. On lightly floured board, knead from 8 to 10 minutes, until dough is smooth and elastic. Put dough in greased bowl, turning to grease all surfaces. Cover with slightly dampened cloth and let rise in a warm place until double in bulk—about 45 minutes. Punch down and let rise again, covered, until almost double in bulk—about 30 to 35 minutes. Punch down again, turn out onto lightly floured board and divide dough into 2 equal parts. With floured rolling pin, roll each part out into an oval, or uneven circle, about 10 inches long. Roll each oval tightly, starting at the wider side and rolling toward you. Roll back and forth to stretch to desired length, putting more pressure on both ends to taper them. Put loaves on greased baking sheets and, with sharp scissors or knife, cut diagonal slit across tops. Let rise in warm place until almost double in bulk—from 1 to 1½ hours. In preheated 400° oven, put a shallow pan of boiling water. On rack above water, bake loaves for 15 minutes. Reduce heat to 350° and bake for 30 minutes more.

If you want your loaves to be shiny, brush them about 5 or 10 minutes before they are due to come out of the oven with one of the following glazes:

1 egg white beaten with 1 Tbs. water, or
1 tsp. cornstarch mixed with 1 tsp. cold water and then with ½ cup boiling water, cooked until smooth and clear and slightly cooled

Sweet Rye Bread

Rising time 8 hours. Set it overnight, if you don't sleep more than 6 hours. *Makes 2 loaves.*

2 cups milk	2 tsp. salt
½ cup skim-milk solids	1 cake compressed yeast, or 1 package dry yeast
¼ cup shortening	
½ cup dark molasses	¼ cup lukewarm water
⅓ cup honey	

2 Tbs. caraway seeds
7¾ cups rye flour
4 Tbs. brewers' yeast
(about) ½ cup regular flour for the board

2 Tbs. vegetable oil (without additives)
1 Tbs. sea salt
2 Tbs. dry yeast (granule form— available at health food stores)
2 Tbs. honey
3 cups warm water

Scald milk and milk solids together and pour over shortening, molasses, honey, and salt in a large bowl. Stir until dissolved and let cool to lukewarm. Soften yeast in ¼ cup lukewarm water and stir into the milk mixture. Add caraway seeds. Combine flour and brewers' yeast and work into the liquids, mixing first with a heavy spoon and then with the hands. Turn out on floured board and knead for 10 to 15 minutes, until dough is smooth and springy but not too stiff. Put dough in a greased bowl, turn dough upside down to grease the top, cover with a clean cloth, and let rise in a warm place until double in bulk. This will take about 6 hours. Punch down, knead again for 3 or 4 minutes on floured board, and shape into 2 round or oval loaves. Put them closely together on a greased baking sheet, cover, and let rise again until double in bulk—about 2 hours this time. Bake at 400° for 15 minutes, reduce heat, and bake at 350° for 35 to 40 minutes more.

Dr. Clive McKay's Triple Rich Cornell Bread

This is a high-protein, high-vitamin, high-mineral bread, restoring many of the nutritional values depleted in the milling of white flour, and vastly improving on ordinary white bread. Moreover, it is perfectly acceptable to the majority of white-bread devotees, many of whom will not accept whole-wheat bread. The Cornell mix itself is simple: in an 8-ounce measuring cup, put in 1 tablespoon of soy flour, 1 teaspoon of wheat germ, and 1 tablespoon of nonfat dry milk powder. Now fill the cup with white flour, preferably unbleached. Thoroughly stirred, this is now used to make a bread which closely resembles ordinary white bread in appearance, but is flavorful and nutritious. It is a perfect way to outflank the family who as yet will not accept whole grains, though its lack of bran keeps it from being a complete substitute for whole wheat. To make the bread, use about 6 cups of well-mixed and sifted Cornell mix. Have on hand:

Soften two tablespoons of the yeast in 3 cups of water. Add the honey. Mix the sea salt with 3 cups of the Cornell mix. When the yeast-honey-water mixture bubbles, gradually add to it the 3 cups of Cornell mix, beating it by hand about 70 or 80 times. You can use an electric mixer, but hand-beaten, it somehow turns out better for me. Now add the 2 tablespoons of oil, and enough of the remaining Cornell mix to form it into a dough which is moderately stiff. Knead this on a flour board, until its texture is smooth and elastic. Then shape it into a ball, place it in a bowl greased with a little oil, and oil the top of the ball.

You are now ready to let it rise: just cover it and put it in a warm place—which doesn't mean oven heat—until it rises to about double the original size. That should take about 45 minutes.

Now use your fist to deflate the ball, fold the edges in, and turn it upside down, letting it rise again for another 20 minutes. Now turn the dough out on the board (which should still be floured). Split the dough into 3 approximately equal parts, and fold each one inward until it is a smooth and tight ball.* Cover these with a cloth, and wait 10 minutes. You are now ready to shape each of the 3 into loaves, and put them in oiled bread pans. In about 45 minutes, the loaves should double in bulk, and you are now ready for baking—325° for 45 minutes, or so. (Vague, because ovens differ in characteristics. 50 minutes may be necessary. The appearance of the loaves will tell you, when you have gained a little experience.)

The recipe should be called: "How to attract small children and keep the wandering husband at home." That isn't theory—this is the special bread we baked for the children at our summer camps. They enjoyed it, and never discovered that we were infiltrating their defenses, and feeding them better nutrition.

*One of these can be used to make rolls, if you wish, as a pleasant change of pace for breakfast.

9
Good-Nutrition Desserts

Contrary to a popularly held unpopular belief, "dessert" is not a forbidden word in the nutritionist's vocabulary. It merely requires definition. Unfortunately, even a conscientious homemaker who makes honest attempts to feed her family sensibly is likely to boggle at a decision about dessert. Should she infuriate her loved ones by serving raw fruit—and raw fruit only? Should she risk alienation, divorce, or runaway children by withholding dessert entirely? Or should she succumb to family brainwashing techniques, toss discretion and nutrition to the winds, and go hog-wild with—oh, dear—sugar?

Needless to say, the author of this cookbook is not going to encourage you to stuff your family with empty calories and nutrient-sabotaging goo. Nor is he going to say, in paraphrase of what might be your rationalizations, "Well, you've virtuously fed your folks a good substantial breakfast, supervised a nutritious lunch, and crammed plenty of vitamins, minerals, and proteins into dinner's main courses. Go ahead—satisfy the yearnings of their sweet little teeth."

On this point I am inflexible. Living and eating should be fun—but not at the expense of health. Rich, sugary desserts in the quantities they are consumed by the American public indict themselves, sooner or later. Along with candy, soda pop, and overstarchy diets, they account in part for this nation's appalling record of obesity, tooth decay, skin disturbances, and a long list of minor to serious illnesses. They do this by direct attack—and more subtly by ruining the appetite for foods which feed the hungry body.

Although the reward-dessert habit can be broken—by feeding larger portions of real food, and sometimes by drastic scenes in which the housewife screams back at her screaming children (including Papa), these are not ideal solutions. In the first place, children (including Papa) who can't possibly finish their vegetables because they're too full, miraculously find room for a 500-calorie half-pound dessert. In the second place, anyone old enough to open the front door unaided is likely to run, not walk, to the nearest candy store to buy a little something sweet to sustain him. So let's not have any delusions. If Mama makes too much fuss without voluntary family cooperation or the honor system, she may breed a houseful of candyholics.

Ingenious and loving ways can be found to pamper a sweet tooth, of course, but the ideal in nutrition is to extract such a tooth from the oral cavity—or at least to deaden its nerve. A sweet tooth does not grow naturally in the mouth. It is an acquisition, useless and often harmful, but nevertheless present in many people for a variety of reasons. (An inordinate craving for sweets should be investigated by the family physician. It may betoken the presence of functional or organic disease, such as hypoglycemia or diabetes.)

It is hardly any wonder that multitudes of Americans grow up to be dessert fetishists. As children they were repeatedly warned—"No dessert until you eat all your spinach," thus making spinach a hateful punishment and dessert a shining reward. The reward image persists in adulthood and gets all mixed up with the emotions. Some people take to drink when their problems (which often include nutritional ones) get too much for them. Others find some satisfaction in stuffing themselves with sweets—"rewards" to compensate for their frustrations, fears, insecurity, and privately suspected inadequacies. Still others use sweets to serve a kind of self-bolstering competitiveness—a way of keeping up with the Joneses. Their reasoning seems to be, "Well, I can't afford a fancy new car, but I *can* eat rich."

Except in rare instances the nutrition-minded American wife and mother is totally unable to convert her family to the ideal and typical European dessert—fresh fruit and cheese, which supply natural sugar and vitamins plus a desirable amount of milk proteins. Oddly enough, a husband may rave about Madame La Parisienne's fruit bowl and cheese tray when invited to this glamorous lady's dinner table. He may smile expansively over his cigar smoke when being entertained by the company's sales manager at a continental restaurant where fruit and cheese are brought to the table with the demitasse and cognac. But try to serve this as a home dessert! The wife who does is usually flattened by husbandly sarcasm or told, not for the first time, that *Mother* thought enough of her boy to bake seven-layer cakes and whipped cream pies every single day.

It does very little good, many a housewife wails, to explain the food facts of life to her household. Her husband, for the most part, is stunned and outraged by the idea that food has any function beyond tasting good and filling his stomach. The children, with wide-eyed innocence and irrefutable logic, are prone to remarks like, "But we're not *hungry* for broiled grapefruit. We're hungry for marshmallow-fudge sundaes—like Tommy's mother gives us."

The nutrition-conscious homemaker should remember that chocolate layer cake usually means 12 to 14 teaspoons of sugar per portion; that baked apples prepared by old-fashioned methods carry more calorie value from sugar than from apples and may mean the loss of about 70 percent of the fruit's vitamin C content. She should remember that the easy-to-use puddings and desserts on supermarket shelves (except on the higher-priced "dietetic" list) are filled with overprocessed starch and sugar, and that even so-called "slimming" prepared gelatin desserts may be up to 85 percent sugar. She should remember, moreover, that the anticipation of a gooey dessert frequently prompts her domestic dinner companions to bypass another helping of foods which do have nourishing qualities.

The end-of-the-meal stumbling block is not insurmountable. Acceptable desserts need not compromise with standards of good nutrition. They need not be dull, and they need not be peculiar. A sweetening agent is usually unavoidable, but all that sweetens is not sugar. There is honey, and there is dark molasses, both of which contain a certain goodness which sugar lacks, even though they are about equal in calories, spoon for spoon, and as injurious to teeth if allowed to remain in the mouth without rinsing. There are also on the market a few satisfactory man-made sweeteners in granular, tablet, or liquid form which contain no sugar—or nutrients either, for that matter. However, they may be used on occasion in place of sugar, either entirely or in part, following the manufacturers' recommendations for proportions.

Despite my reputation as a stormy critic of overprocessed foods, it is not sugar itself (or alone) which is my target. It is, rather, the public's avid consumption of unbelievably excessive quantities of sugar which rouses my ire—and sympathies. Sugar is no nutritional bugaboo when it is used as a condiment in discreet amounts or even, sometimes, in amounts which seem to exceed discretion, provided the rest of the day's meals have supplied adequate intake of nutrients and provided also that the dessert which includes sugar includes also elements which contribute to total nutrition.

Gelatin Desserts

Sugarless Whipped Gelatin Dessert

1 envelope unflavored whole gelatin
¼ cup cold water
½ cup skim-milk solids
hot water

1 cup sugar-free carbonated soda —any favorite fruit or berry flavor
1 egg white
½ tsp. vanilla

Soften gelatin in ¼ cup cold water. Put skim-milk solids in a measuring cup and stir in enough hot water to yield a cupful of milk. Dissolve softened gelatin in milk and add 1 cup of sugar-free carbonated soda. Stir to blend well; then chill in refrigerator until firm. Add vanilla and whip mixture until frothy. Beat egg white until stiff and fold into the whipped gelatin. Return to refrigerator until firm. Serve as is, or with topping of fresh or frozen fruit or berries—unsweetened. *Serves 4.*

Homemade Gelatin Dessert

2 Tbs. unflavored gelatin
½ cup cold water
½ cup boiling water
3 cups fresh, frozen, or canned fruit juice sweetened to taste if necessary with sugarless sweetener, honey, or brown sugar

(1 cup sliced fresh, frozen, or canned fruit or berries*)

Soften gelatin in cold water; then add the solution to boiling water and stir until dissolved. Add fruit juice, blend thoroughly, and pour into molds or cups which have been rinsed with cold water. Firm in refrigerator. If this is to be served plain, let it set thoroughly. If you are going to add fruit, do so when the jelly is only half firm. *Serves 4 to 6.*

Fresh or frozen-fresh pineapple (not canned) must be boiled for 2 or 3 minutes before it is added to gelatin.

Custards

Good-Nutrition "Boiled" Custard

4 egg yolks
2 Tbs. brown sugar
2 Tbs. dark molasses or honey
⅛ tsp. salt

2 cups milk
⅓ cup skim-milk solids
flavoring (see end of recipe)

Stir egg yolks with a fork until blended but not frothy. Add sweetener and salt, and stir. Scald milk and milk solids together, add slowly to egg mixture, and stir or beat until all ingredients are well blended. Pour mixture into a heavy-bottomed saucepan and stir over low heat until it thickens—5 to 7 minutes, depending on how you interpret "low heat." There are two ways to determine when custard has cooked enough: (1) when it coats the spoon or (2) when a cooking thermometer reads 175°. When one of these two things happens, remove pan from stove, allow custard to cool slightly, and then chill it in refrigerator. A few minutes before serving, flavor custard by stirring in your choice of:

1 tsp. vanilla, maple, or rum flavoring
1 tsp. lemon juice
½ tsp. almond extract

If you like, add also ½ cup grated or shredded cocoanut. This is a soft custard, not firm, and may be served alone or mixed with fresh, frozen, or canned fruit, or it may be spooned over small servings of ice cream or good-nutrition puddings or cake. *Serves 4.*

Note: For a coffee-flavored custard, add 1 tablespoon instant coffee or instant coffee substitute to scalded milk before beating.

Good-Nutrition Baked Custard

3 cups milk
½ cup skim-milk solids
4 whole eggs or 6 egg yolks
2 Tbs. brown sugar
2 Tbs. dark molasses or honey
1 tsp. vanilla (or ½ tsp. almond extract)

⅛ tsp. salt
butter or margarine for greasing custard cups
nutmeg, cinnamon, shredded cocoanut, or finely ground nuts for garnish

Scald milk and milk solids together. Beat eggs or yolks with a fork and add sweeteners, vanilla or almond extract, and salt. Pour scalded milk over these ingredients slowly, stirring constantly. Do not beat. Pour into lightly greased custard cups to within ¼ inch of top, and sprinkle with garnish. Set cups in large, flat baking pan partly filled with hot water. Cups should rest in water to the halfway mark. Bake at 300° for 35 to 40 minutes, until a stainless steel knife, inserted in the center of one cup, comes out clean. Serve warm or chilled in cups—or inverted on dessert plates and surrounded with fresh, frozen, or canned fruit. *Makes 4 large or 6 small servings.*

Note: For better nutrition and a pleasantly nutty taste, add 4 to 6 tablespoons of wheat germ to the mixture before you pour it into the custard cups, stirring to distribute evenly.

Puddings

Fruit Tapioca Pudding

Processed tapioca is no prize, but the addition of eggs, skim-milk solids, and fruit can make nutritional sense out of this old favorite.

½ cup skim-milk solids	sugar—or 1 tsp. sugarless liquid sweetener
2¾ cups whole or skim milk	⅛ tsp. salt
2 eggs, separated	½ tsp. vanilla
4 Tbs. quick-cooking tapioca	1–2 cups diced fresh, frozen, or canned fruit—or berries
2 Tbs. brown	

Add milk solids to either whole or skim milk and scald. Beat egg yolks slightly with a fork and add to scalded milk. Stir in tapioca, sweetener, and salt. Cook over moderate heat or in double boiler for about 10 minutes, stirring frequently. Do not let it boil. Remove from heat and let cool slightly. Stir in vanilla. Beat egg whites until stiff and fold into tapioca mixture. Chill and serve topped with fruit. *Serves 4 to 6.*

Old-Fashioned Custardy Rice Pudding

2 eggs	1 cup seedless raisins
½ cup skim-milk solids	1¼ cups cooked rice (preferably brown, but at least converted)
1⅔ cups whole milk	
2 Tbs. each of dark molasses and honey—or 4 of brown sugar	
¼ tsp. salt	¼ tsp. mixed cinnamon and nutmeg
1 tsp. vanilla	

Beat eggs. Combine milk solids with milk, add eggs, and beat again. Add sweetener, salt, vanilla, raisins, and rice, and stir until sugar is dissolved (if you're using sugar) or until molasses and honey are well distributed. Pour into a greased casserole and sprinkle top with mixed spices. Put casserole in a shallow pan of hot water; bake at 325° until a stainless steel knife, inserted at the center, comes out clean—about 30 minutes. *Serves 4.*

Brown Rice and Molasses Pudding

1 cup skim-milk solids	¼ cup wheat germ
5 cups milk	2 Tbs. butter or margarine
2 egg yolks	½ tsp. vanilla
½ tsp. salt	1 cup chopped dates, chopped mixed dried fruits, or raisins
4–6 Tbs. dark molasses	
½ tsp. ginger	
1 cup brown rice	

Dissolve milk solids in milk, and beat in egg yolks, salt, molasses, and ginger. Heat in top of double boiler until hot—not boiling—and slowly add rice and wheat germ. Stir, cover, and steam over simmering water for 1 hour, until rice is tender. Stir in butter and vanilla. Drop chopped fruit into 1 cup of boiling water, reduce heat, and simmer for 5 minutes. Drain and stir fruit into rice mixture. Serve hot or cold, with or without crushed fruit. *Serves 6 to 8.*

Brown Rice Apple Pudding

2 cups cooked brown rice	½ cup raisins
2 eggs, separated	4 medium-sized sweet apples
¼ tsp. salt	3 Tbs. butter or margarine, melted
¾ tsp. cinnamon	
⅓ cup brown sugar	

Combine cooked rice with beaten egg yolks, salt, cinnamon, sugar, and raisins. Slice or chop unpeeled apples very fine and add to mixture. Fold in beaten egg whites. Stir in melted butter and pour pudding into well-greased baking dish. Bake at 350° for 30 minutes. *Serves 4 to 6.*

Good-as-Gold Vegetable Pudding

2 cups peeled, diced raw sweet potatoes,	carrots, winter squash, or pumpkin

3 cups salted water
   (½ teaspoon salt)
½ cup undeger-
   minated yellow
   corn meal
3 cups milk
½ cup skim-milk
   solids

¾ cup dark molasses
½ tsp. salt
1 Tbs. butter or
   margarine
¼ tsp. each cinnamon,
   ginger and nutmeg
⅛ tsp. ground cloves
½ cup seedless raisins

Cook diced vegetables in salted water until soft. Drain, reserving water, and mash. Bring 2 cups of the vegetable water to boil and slowly add corn meal, stirring. Reduce heat and cook, stirring, until thickened. Add and mix well the mashed vegetables, milk with milk solids, molasses, salt, butter, spices, and raisins. Pour into a greased baking dish and bake at 325° for 1 hour. *Serves 6 to 8.*

Indian Pudding

Not authentic Indian, but a good way to get eggs, whole grains, and wheat germ into your papooses.

4 slices crustless
   whole-wheat
   bread
2 Tbs. butter or
   margarine
4 Tbs. wheat germ
2 eggs

¼ tsp. salt
4 Tbs. dark
   molasses
2½ cups milk
¼ cup skim-milk
   solids

Spread bread with butter or margarine. Put slices in greased baking dish and sprinkle generously with wheat germ. Beat together all remaining ingredients and pour over the bread. Bake at 300° for 1 hour. *Serves 4.*

Cottage Cheese Soufflé Pudding

3 Tbs. butter or
   margarine, melted
3 Tbs. whole-wheat
   or unbleached flour
½ tsp. salt
1 cup warm milk
2 Tbs. skim-milk
   solids

3 eggs, separated
4 Tbs. brown sugar
2 Tbs. lemon juice
1 tsp. grated lemon
   rind
½ cup seedless raisins
1 cup cottage cheese
2 Tbs. wheat germ

Blend butter, flour, and salt to a smooth paste. Combine milk with milk solids and add slowly, stirring until no lumps remain. Cook in top of double boiler until thickened and smooth, and remove from heat. Beat egg yolks; add sugar, lemon juice, and rind; and stir. Add egg mixture to sauce and stir; then add raisins and cottage cheese, and stir or beat until very

smooth. Beat egg whites stiff and fold into mixture. Pour into well-greased baking dish, sprinkle with wheat germ, place dish in pan of hot water, and bake at 350° until set—about 30 to 40 minutes. *Serves 4 to 6.*

Good-Nutrition Fruit Desserts

Brown Betty

Apples are traditional for this pudding, but it may be made with other fruits—either alone or combined. Frozen, stewed, or canned apricots or peaches are nice, using the fruit juice in place of the lemon juice and water called for in the following recipe.

1 cup whole-wheat
   bread crumbs or
   graham cracker
   crumbs
½ cup wheat germ
¼ cup butter or
   margarine, melted
2½ cups sliced apples
   (with or without
   peels)

½ cup seedless
   raisins
2 Tbs. honey
⅓ cup brown sugar
¾ tsp. cinnamon
¼ tsp. nutmeg
⅛ tsp. cloves
½ tsp. salt
1 Tbs. lemon juice in
   ¼ cup water

Combine crumbs, wheat germ, and melted butter. Cover bottom of a lightly greased baking dish with about one-third of this mixture. Sprinkle apples and raisins, combined, with honey and toss lightly to distribute evenly. In another bowl combine sugar with spices and salt, mixing well. Put half of the honeyed apple-raisin mixture over crumbs in baking dish, and sprinkle with half of the sugar-spice mixture and half of the lemon water. Cover with another layer (one-third) of the crumb mixture, then with the rest of the apples. Sprinkle with remaining sugar-spice mixture and again with lemon water. Top with final one-third of crumbs. Cover baking dish and bake at 350° for 35 minutes. Remove cover, increase oven heat to 400°, and brown for 10 to 15 minutes. Serve hot with custard sauce (page 71), cream, or sour cream. *Serves 4 to 6.*

Fruit Pan Dowdy

2 cups sliced
   naturally sweet
   apples, peaches,
   apricots, or
   nectarines

2 Tbs. brown sugar
¼ tsp. each salt,
   nutmeg, and
   cinnamon
½ cup hot fruit juice

½ recipe wheat-germ biscuit dough (page 60) or shortcake

biscuit dough (page 60)

Spread sliced fruit over bottom of well-greased baking dish. Mix sugar with seasonings and sprinkle over fruit. Pour hot fruit juice over this and bake at 400° for 10 to 15 minutes, until fruit is tender. Remove from oven. Pat or roll biscuit dough to proper size and cover fruit. Return to 400° oven and bake 15 to 20 minutes, until dough rises and browns. *Serves 4 to 6.*

Good-Nutrition Baked Apples

4 large, firm apples	1 Tbs. butter, melted
2 Tbs. honey	1 Tbs. orange or
2 Tbs. wheat germ	lemon juice

Scrub and dry apples. Core them carefully without cutting through the bottoms, and peel only the tops—removing about 1 inch of the peel. Put them in a baking dish. Combine honey, wheat germ, melted butter, and juice, and fill hollows of the apples with this mixture. Sprinkle with cinnamon or nutmeg. Preheat oven to 400°. Add ¼ cup of boiling water to the baking dish and bake the apples only until they are tender, basting occasionally. They should not bake for more than 30 minutes, and some varieties will be tender in 15 minutes. Serve hot or cold, with or without cream, sour cream, or whipped cream. *Serves 4.*

Good-Nutrition Frozen Desserts

Freezer Pops

Many a child has been switched from sugary ice pops to Mom's clever substitutes: In individual plastic ice cube cups, or in plastic trays out of which you can press a single cube, pour any natural fruit juice your child likes—orange, pineapple, berry, mixed-fruit, etc. Place a pop stick or small drinking straw in a corner of each cup and let it rest on the outer rim. (Several doctors' wives I know use narrow tongue depressors for the sticks.) Freeze.

These are popular with children in warm weather, especially since you need not put maternal restrictions on the number they can have. (Why is it children always seem to ask, "Can I have two?") Each pop represents only a small portion of what would in its original form be a glass of fruit juice. Older children soon learn to make their own out of favorite fresh, reconstituted frozen, or canned fruit juices—a pleasant form of parental permissiveness. Puréed baby fruits can also be used, although the juices go further and contain less added sugar, or none at all.

"Ice Cream" Pops

Children who balk at drinking milk will accept these. For an ice cube trayful, mix ½ cup skim-milk solids with 1 cup whole milk and flavor with vanilla, fruit juice, a little chocolate syrup, instant cocoa, or—treat of treats—instant decaffeinated coffee. You may be able to get away without adding sweetener. If not, sweeten the mixture before pouring into the trays with honey or dark molasses. Freeze as in preceding recipe for Freezer Pops.

Sugarless Fruit Sherbet

two 6-oz. cans unsweetened frozen juice concentrate (orange, pineapple, grape, berry, etc., singly or in combination)	3½ cups cold water 2 Tbs. liquid sugarless sweetener 1 cup skim-milk solids

Put all ingredients in a large bowl (or electric mixer, if you have one) and beat vigorously until well blended. Pour into ice cube trays or flat dishes and freeze only until mushy—about 1 hour. Return to chilled mixing bowl and beat at low speed until soft, then at high speed until creamy—about 3 to 5 minutes. Pour into trays or dishes again and freeze. Serve in chilled sherbet glasses or dessert dishes topped with crushed fruit or berries. *Makes about 1½ quarts.*

Sugarless Frozen Custard

1¼ cups milk	½ cup cold water
½ cup evaporated milk	1 Tbs. liquid sugarless sweetener
2 tsp. unflavored whole gelatin	2 tsp. vanilla*
½ cup skim-milk solids	½ cup ice water

For other flavors, omit vanilla. Before second freezing, beat ½ to 1 cup any mashed or puréed fruit or ½ cup banana flakes. For coffee custard, add 1 tablespoon instant regular or decaffeinated coffee to scalded milk.

Combine milk and evaporated milk, and scald. Remove from heat. Soften gelatin in cold water and add to scalded milk. Add sweetener and vanilla, and stir well, until thoroughly mixed. Pour into ice cube trays and cool to room temperature. When cool, freeze until center is mushy (edges may be frozen). Pour into chilled bowl and beat at low speed until smooth and creamy. In separate chilled bowl dissolve milk solids in ice water and beat vigorously until it has the consistency of whipped cream. Fold whipped milk into former mixture, return to trays, and freeze until firm. *Makes about 1 quart.*

Honey-Berry Ice Cream

2 cups strawberries, raspberries, or blackberries	½ cup whipping cream—or ½ cup skim-milk solids and ½ cup ice water
⅓ cup milk	
2 Tbs. honey	

Mash or purée berries, stir in milk and honey, and blend thoroughly. Pour into ice cube trays and freeze until mushy. Pour into chilled bowl and beat at low speed until smooth and creamy. Whip cream—or dissolve skim-milk solids in ice water and beat until it has the consistency of whipped cream. Fold into fruit mixture, return to trays, and freeze—or freeze in sherbet glasses if these are heavy (thin ones may crack in the freezer). *Makes about 1½ pints.*

Good-Nutrition Cakes

As with everything else you cook, the choice is yours when you bake a cake. You can concentrate on its gorgeous height, its perfect symmetry, its fine texture, and its melt-in-your-mouth sweetness—or you can consider its contribution to good diet.

You know by now that I am not happy about the amount of white flour and white sugar consumed by the American public—even that part of it which says, indignantly, "I never use sugar!" The individual who may not so much as put a sugar bowl on the table nevertheless manages to swallow more than a hundred pounds of it a year. You doubt this? Please refer to my earlier book, *Low Blood Sugar and You,* published by Grosset & Dunlap, in which you will find a great deal of information about the unsuspected ways in which high sugar intake is causing illness for us; and a table listing the sugar content of many popular foods. For example, there is ½ teaspoon of sugar in a stick of chewing gum—and there are 15 teaspoons of sugar in a single serving of frosted chocolate cake. There are 3 to 5 teaspoons of sugar in a 6-ounce glass of cola or carbonated soda pop—and up to 7 teaspoons per small-sized candy bar.

While you'd expect to find sugar in generous amounts in these and other foods classified as "sweets," which you say you never eat, there is a surprising quantity of it in many foods not classified as sweets—in canned vegetables, for example, and frozen heat-and-serve main courses or complete dinners, in commercial bread and rolls and breakfast cereals. In addition, restaurant patrons unwittingly eat enormous amounts of sugar. It seems that when a chef, like a food processor, is stumped for a condiment to add to a recipe to ensure its palatability, his reflexes move his arm automatically toward the sugar bin. There is sugar in restaurant and cafeteria gravies, stews, pot roasts, meat loaves, casseroles, spaghetti sauces, and some creamed vegetables.

My opinion of white flour can be found elsewhere in this book, preceding the bread section.

Except for the dedicated gourmet crowd and determined seekers after truly optimum nutrition (the two are not necessarily mutually exclusive), American housewives who bake the family's cakes from scratch are becoming as scarce as their sisters who bake the family's bread—which is to say, they're vanishing like the American whooping crane.

Yet, who can blame the millions of busy homemakers for turning to prepared cake mixes as naturally and gratefully as flowers turn their faces to the sun? Cleverly and delectably compounded, these mixes are attractively packaged and found on supermarket shelves in such mouth-watering variety as to make flour sifting and resifting, shortening blending, and endless beating as old hat as bending over a washboard. As further seduction, several of the cake-mix companies include in their packages disposable cake pans or mixing bags. Not even any bowls to wash! And to make absolutely certain the home cook is freed of further decision and responsibility, some companies offer ready-to-mix ingredients for frostings.

While I cannot quarrel with streamlined techniques which improve the lot of the busy housewife, I can and do quarrel with any food whose repeated use at the expense of good nutrition may impose hidden or deferred taxes on the body's well-being. The run-of-the-mill commercial cake mix is composed of refined white flour, refined white sugar, and not-so-refined artificial flavorings and colorings. There is, to be sure, some sort of enrichment program afoot, and "enriched" has become a magic word even on cake mix boxes. The word has about as much real meaning as the word "large" on a can of olives. To get really large olives, you have to look for the word "jumbo." To get really enriched cake, you do one simple thing: Make your own cakes from recipes with ingredients whose nutrient values are intact, which do not rely heavily on sugar for palatability, and on synthetic preservatives, dyes, and artificial flavors.

Except for gingerbread, spice, and other dark cakes, making a cake out of whole-wheat flour may seem a little on the odd side to the eyes—if not the taste—of people accustomed to airy-fairy angel-food and other pale cakes. And while not even this adamant antagonist of white sugar will try to make you bake all your cakes without any sugar at all, you will be asked to try brown sugar and, in some recipes, to replace some of the sugar with molasses or honey. (It is also possible to use sugarless sweeteners for cake baking, and the pharmaceutical houses which manufacture the sweeteners to be found on any dietetic shelf will be delighted to send you their recipe booklets. See also Where to Find Special-purpose Foods, page 11.)

Stir sugar into orange juice and cook over low heat, stirring, until sugar is dissolved. Continue to cook without stirring until mixture becomes syrupy, forming a thread when a small amount is dropped from a spoon. Remove from heat. Resift—at least 4 times—the flour with cream of tartar and salt. Separate the eggs and beat the yolks well. Add lemon juice and beat again. Beat the egg whites until stiff but not dry; then slowly beat in the sugar-orange syrup and extract. Add yolk mixture to dry ingredients; then fold in the beaten egg whites. Pour into an ungreased angel cake pan, "cut" the batter with a knife to eliminate air bubbles, and bake at 375° for 15 minutes. Reduce heat to 250° and bake 15 to 20 minutes longer. Remove pan from oven and invert on rack or trivet. Let it cool for at least 1 hour before removing the cake from the pan.

Wheat-Germ Butter Layer Cake

1½ cups sifted whole-wheat pastry flour	3 tsp. wheat germ
	½ cup butter
	1 cup sugar
3 tsp. baking powder	3 eggs
	1 cup milk
¼ tsp salt	½ tsp. vanilla, almond, or maple extract
½ cup skim-milk solids	

Resift flour with baking powder, salt, and milk solids. Stir wheat germ into mixture, distributing it evenly. Cream butter and sugar. Stir eggs into milk with a fork. Combine flour mixture with creamed sugar and liquid, and beat with 250 strokes by hand or 2½ minutes in electric mixer. Stir flavoring into batter. Pour into 2 lined or greased-and-floured layer cake pans and bake at 350° for 35 minutes. Remove from pans; cool on rack or trivet. Spread one layer with custard sauce (page 71) with added slices of naturally sweet fresh or frozen fruit or berries. Top with second layer.

Sunburned Angel Cake

1½ cups brown sugar	¼ tsp. salt
½ cup strained orange juice	8 eggs
1 cup sifted whole-wheat pastry flour	1 Tbs. strained lemon juice
¾ tsp. cream of tartar	½ tsp. vanilla or almond extract

Oatmeal Spice Cake

2 cups boiling water	4 tsp. wheat germ
1 cup seedless raisins	1 cup brown sugar
1 cup oatmeal	2½ tsp. baking powder
1 cup sifted whole-wheat flour	½ tsp. each cinnamon, nutmeg, cloves

| ¼ cup skim-milk solids | 1 egg |
| ½ cup solid shortening | 1 cup milk or buttermilk |

Pour boiling water over raisins to plump them; then drain and reserve. Combine all dry ingredients and mix thoroughly. Cut in shortening with pastry blender or two knives. Stir egg into milk and add to flour mixture. Beat to blend thoroughly, stir in raisins, and pour into lined or greased-and-floured cake pan. Bake at 350° for 40 minutes.

Graham Cracker Cake

1 cup brown sugar	2 tsp. baking powder
½ cup solid shortening	¼ tsp. salt
2 eggs, beaten	¾ cup graham cracker crumbs
1 cup sifted whole-wheat flour	2 tsp. wheat germ
	1 cup milk
¼ cup skim-milk solids	½ tsp. vanilla, almond or maple extract

Cream sugar and shortening together. Stir in beaten eggs; then beat until very well blended. Resift flour with milk solids, baking powder, and salt; then stir into mixture the crumbs and wheat germ, distributing evenly. To creamed sugar add flour mixture alternately with liquid, stirring to blend. Stir in flavoring. Pour into lined shallow cake pans and bake at 350° for 30 minutes. Serve squares topped with custard sauce, fresh or frozen fruit or berries, or whipped topping.

Nut Cake

⅓ cup softened butter or margarine	¼ cup skim-milk solids
½ cup brown sugar	2 tsp. baking powder
½ cup dark molasses	½ tsp. salt
½ cup milk	¼ cup wheat germ
½ tsp. vanilla	1 cup broken nut meats
2 eggs	
1 cup whole-wheat flour	

Cream butter with sugar. Add molasses, milk, vanilla, and unbeaten eggs, and stir to blend well. Sift flour with milk solids, baking powder, and salt, and stir into this mixture the wheat germ, distributing evenly. Combine flour mixture with liquid, stirring to mix well.

Fold in nuts. Pour into lined or greased-and-floured loaf pan and bake at 375° for 45 minutes.

Honey-Molasses Spice Cake

¾ cup honey	½ cup skim-milk solids
½ cup dark molasses	
¼ cup softened butter	2½ tsp. baking powder
¼ cup softened shortening	½ tsp. salt
	1 tsp. cinnamon
2 eggs, separated	½ tsp. each nutmeg and cloves
1 cup milk	
1½ cups sifted whole-wheat flour (½ cup may be soybean flour)	2 tsp. wheat germ
	1 Tbs. cold water

Combine honey, molasses, butter, and shortening. Add egg yolks and beat until blended. Add milk slowly, stirring to mix thoroughly. Resift flour with milk solids, baking powder, salt, and spices, and add to milk mixture, stirring only enough to moisten and blend ingredients. Beat egg whites with 1 tablespoon of cold water until stiff but not dry, and fold into batter. Pour into lined or greased-and-floured cake pan and bake at 350° for 40 minutes.

Upside Down Cake

2 cups sifted whole-wheat flour	4 Tbs. solid shortening
3 tsp. baking powder	¾ cup milk
¼ cup skim-milk solids	1 egg, beaten
¾ cup brown sugar	4 Tbs. melted butter
¼ tsp. salt	1 tsp. cinnamon
3 tsp. wheat germ	1 Tbs. cream
	3 large apples, cored and sliced*

Resift flour with baking powder, milk solids, *2 tablespoons* of the sugar, and salt. Stir in wheat germ. Cut in shortening with pastry blender or two knives until mixture is mealy. Combine milk and beaten egg and stir into flour mixture, blending to a soft dough. Set this aside while you combine melted butter with remaining brown sugar, cinnamon, and cream. Spread the sugar mixture over the bottom of a well-greased cake pan. Press apple slices firmly into this in a single layer. Spread re-

Make this also with fresh peaches or apricots—or canned peaches, apricots, or pineapple.

served dough evenly over the fruit. Bake at 350° for 50 to 60 minutes.

Honey Fruit Cake

1 cup each seedless raisins, chopped dates, chopped figs	whole-wheat flour
¼ cup butter	1 tsp. cinnamon
1½ cups honey	½ tsp. each, ginger and cloves
½ cup brown sugar	4 tsp. wheat germ
½ cup water	1 cup chopped or broken nuts
·3 cups sifted	

Combine fruit, butter, honey, sugar, and water, and simmer over low heat for 10 minutes. Remove from heat and cool to room temperature. Sift flour with spices and stir in wheat germ, distributing evenly. Add sweetened fruit mixture and nuts, mixing well. Bake in very well-greased pans at 300° for 1½ hours.

Refrigerator Cheese Cake

2 Tbs. unflavored whole gelatin	1 tsp. grated orange or lemon rind
½ cup cold water	1 tsp. vanilla
2 egg yolks	½ cup skim-milk solids
½ cup sugar	
½ cup milk	½ cup ice water
1 tsp. salt	2 egg whites
2 cups cottage cheese	½ cup graham cracker crumbs
½ cup sour cream or yogurt	
3 Tbs. orange or lemon juice	2 tsp. wheat germ

Soak gelatin in cold water and set aside. In saucepan or double boiler combine egg yolks, sugar, milk, and salt. Stir over low heat or boiling water until thickened. Remove from heat and add gelatin solution, stirring until it is dissolved. Chill this mixture in refrigerator, or by putting pan in another pan of ice water. Combine cottage cheese, sour cream, juice, rind, and vanilla, and beat until smooth. Add cheese mixture to the chilled custard mixture and stir until blended. In chilled bowl, mix milk solids with ice water and beat until it is the consistency of whipped cream. Beat egg whites until stiff but not dry. Fold into the cheese mixture

first the whipped milk, then the egg whites. Pour into a glass pie or cake pan. Combine graham cracker crumbs and wheat germ and sprinkle over top. Refrigerate for several hours before serving.

Cake Frostings

Please don't ruin a carefully nutrition-guarded cake by smearing it with an icing made by using the usual 1, 2, or 3 cups of sugar! Best of all, of course, would be cake with no icing at all—a taste that can be acquired. For those who insist on gilding the lily, however, here are three frostings which do not lean too heavily on sugar for their appeal.

White or Tinted Frosting

2 Tbs. cream or strong coffee	3 Tbs. butter
	½ cup powdered sugar
2 tsp. vanilla—or 1 tsp. almond or maple extract	¾ cup skim-milk solids

Combine ingredients and beat vigorously until smooth and creamy.

Cream Cheese Frosting

2 packages (6 oz.) cream cheese	1½ tsp. grated orange or lemon rind
1½ Tbs. sweet or sour cream	½ tsp. vanilla, almond, or rum extract
⅔ cup confectioners' sugar	

Cream the cheese and cream together, working with a fork until mixture is soft and fluffy. Gradually beat in the sugar; then add and beat in the rind and flavoring.

Honey Frosting

1 cup honey	2 egg whites

Boil honey for 10 minutes, until a cooking thermometer reads 238°. Remove from heat and allow to cool for 10 minutes. Beat egg whites until stiff. Pour honey very slowly over beaten egg whites while continuing to beat, until mixture is thick. Let cool before spreading over cake.

Index